For my family, friends, and the multitude of people I've only ever met online.

WE MET IN THE FORUMS

ROB ULITSKI

We Met In The Forums

Published by Pastel Wasteland

First Edition: April 2024

Sign up and keep up to date with Rob's latest work at:

www.robhorror.com

@robulitski

Cover Photo by Min An from Pexels

Editing + Titles by Rob Ulitski

ACKNOWLEDGMENTS

None of this would have been possible without my family and friends. The journey to this point has been a thrilling ride, and I've put more of myself into this book than any of my previous stories.

Special thanks to Bekah for always being the first to read and offer her advice, Alex for his help getting the story into shape, and to Joseph for his proofreading mastery.

And to my hometown of Portsmouth. Thank you for inspiring a large part of this book, both good and bad. Never change.

PROLOGUE

2019

We met in the forums.

A world away from the world outside, a place where anonymous desires and opinions replaced everyday niceties and small talk. A world where mind came first and flesh came second.

In the forums, I was a string of characters without a home—lines of computer code working together to light up the screen in shapes I'd formed in my head seconds prior. Limitless ideas, ideologies, thoughts and feelings, cascading in branches of mysterious questions from mysterious strangers.

In the forums, words were king, and I'd learned that anything goes, as long as you can put that anything into words. I'd become a master of describing illusory thoughts and feelings.

I logged in for hours and hours every day, melting the time between studying and partying with a menagerie of ideas and arguments and outcast points of view. I'd partake in this dance of words with anyone who wanted to join in, discussing almost anything as long as it was interesting and I had a way to explain my unique viewpoint on it.

Politics were boring, dichotomous. I yearned for the conversations in between, the perspectives that weren't only unusual, but challenging. *What do you think about the look in people's eyes when they're about to perish? What is the one thing that would get you cancelled if you revealed your true thoughts about it?*

People were most interesting when stripped bare and twisted inside out; that's when you could really see what they were made of. Most people worked so hard to keep up appearances, keep their armoured flesh sealed to protect themselves. I hung around to find the people on the edge, the ones who would eventually come to me bleeding and ready to show me their rotten organs and all the disgusting things they kept hidden from the real world.

Most people came and went. We'd discuss death or conspiracies or the weird routines of serial killers and how there was always the one kill that gave up the whole gig. But then they'd get bored, crave some beige conversations about TV episodes or schoolwork or how sexy that one pornstar with the massive dick on Onlyfans is. Then I'd lose interest. Go from burning red to a mellow blue, move on without a thought. They'd run back to try and recapture the heat from our taboo conversations, but we'd never burn that bright again.

But then I found Leo. Or he found me. Initially, I didn't

know Leo by name. I knew him by a string of characters: **u/LE02019xyk.** Leo almost got banned from one page for asking why we didn't hold many open casket funerals in the UK. He'd been to one abroad and loved spending time with the corpse, prodding and squishing the body to see the way in which the skin would contort around his fingers, inhaling the saccharine scent of post-death. He said you could probably dig a finger or two into an eye socket and feel the space the brain had occupied for a whole existence, birth to death.

As a concept, you had to admit it was pretty interesting. These dearly departed folk are basically set dressing for an expensive party, where the soul has moved on (either to a blank abyss or a happy party in the clouds, depending which way you lean on religion), and so this shell of a person is just propped up over by the buffet, watching as Aunt Jean stuffs another five cheese straws into her gullet as a 'treat' before Tuesday's slimming club.

Leo came ready-built with plenty of these challenging thought experiments in tow, and I couldn't help but look forward to talking to him every day. I didn't know anything about him as a person, in the real world, but on the forums, he was some kind of deity I just couldn't get enough of. Talking to him felt like talking to God, but also to myself, which raised questions about my mental state, but that wasn't anything to think too deeply on.

My string of characters looked like this: **u/Joshx4265ab.** The numbers at the end didn't really mean anything, but I got used to them. They became me, and I became them.

— — — —

— u/ Josh4265ab

I don't really know what I feel about that. I don't think suicide is the only way out of a bad mental health situation. But I also think that we can examine these things all of our lives and still get to the end without any fucking idea about what we wanted or felt.

-

——— u/ LE02019xyk

True true. But I think that being of sound mind your whole life would be boring though. Like, if everything just went right 100% of the time? I don't think I'd be into it.

-

— u/ Josh4265ab

How so?

-

——— u/ LE02019xyk

Picture it this way. When you're starving, that first bite of food feels like heaven, right? The best thing ever? But if you're eating things the whole day, and keeping your stomach at a level place, that same bite would be much less amazing. It would just be 'meh' you know?

-

— u/ Josh4265ab

I think I get you.

-

——— u/ LE02019xyk

Kind of like when you really want to fuck a girl and you imagine all those different sensations when you're dancing close to her at a club. And when it finally happens, it's fireworks. But ten years down the line, when you want to fuck, it happens between washing dishes or putting the kids to bed, and it's great but also not great. Does that make sense?

-

— **u/ Josh4265ab**

I don't fuck girls. But I do get what you mean.

-

—— **u/ LE02019xyk**

Is fucking guys fun?

— — — —

2020

We had an online anniversary for our one-year friendship. We lit up the forums with some risky questions, everything from which member of our families we'd sacrifice first, through to which local retiree we'd let suck our cocks. And then we sat back and laughed at the comments, DMing each other on the chat as we did every day. We were still to share a single word over the phone or away from the platform, but I didn't really mind that at all. We were just two people connected by some interests—and probably undiagnosed mental illnesses—and we were having the time of our lives.

At home, at university, I was one guy. Josh. 19. Cute face, brown hair, always high off cheap weed. Good at taking photos, doing a degree in it whilst I worked out what I really wanted to do, and what mould I fit into. But on the forums, I was another. Still Josh. Still 19. But I was a buzzing energy, a force to be reckoned with, someone who had intelligent thoughts on a variety of different subjects. I don't know if it was the platform that made me feel that way, or if it was Leo, but I knew that I loved the contrast of my life online and life in the real world. I didn't really care back then if the two personas crossed over or merged or whatever.

— — — —

—— u/ LE02019xyk
Happy one year friend-versary.
-
— u/ Josh4265ab
Is that a thing?
-
—— u/ LE02019xyk
It is now.
-
— u/ Josh4265ab
Cool.
-
—— u/ LE02019xyk
Remember when you said about fucking guys. Does it ever feel like you're fucking yourself?

2021

Knee deep in the pandemic, I was terminally online. Things went a bit shit on the outside, but between the dark room, my PC, and the forums, I was getting through it. The world was red hot and scary but the forums were still black and white. Words on white, shapes on-screen. My discussions became equally more and less exciting.

I discussed the boring things with a lot of strangers. What I was up to. Who I talked to on video call each day. What I was doing for work and money.

I discussed the exciting things with strangers too. The idea of a new black death, a plague spreading with no kind of plan or M.O. People were dying. A lot of people. I thought that was sad but poetic.

Leo went offline for a couple of days. That just felt sad. He explained he'd lost someone. I reached out a metaphorical hand and said I was there if he needed to chat. He accepted it but at a distance.

After all, we were just digital ideas on a platform. We'd still never talked in person. Or on video call. Or phone.

That changed late 2021. Early morning, with university deadlines looming, we were so busy watching video lessons and trying to communicate in little boxes on-screen, that it was easy to let the real world slip away. Some days, it seemed like the screen would be the only thing left once the world was decimated by disease. What a boring way for us all to expire.

The sun was bright and orange even though the balding weatherman promised snow. The world was weird—the weather was surely following in step.

I'd logged on at 10:01am. I had a message at 10:02am. He was waiting for me to be online.

— — — —

Would it be weird to chat on the phone?

-

— u/ Josh4265ab

I don't think so. I might be underwhelming or something though…

-

—— u/ LE02019xyk

That's okay. I just need a friendly voice.

— — — —

We exchanged numbers and moments later his name appeared on my screen. Incoming call.

It was weird to start with, but we relaxed into it easily, just like we had on the forums. He explained that I meant a lot to him as a friend, and he was worried that talking in real life might break that facade. But, if anything, it brought us closer. We were real people talking, flesh and blood, not just personalities diluted through pixels. Until:

"My brother died. It came out of nowhere."

It was such an intimate thing to share with a stranger. In the cold light of day and exposed by the sickly orange light spilling through the slits of my blinds, it certainly felt heavier than I was expecting. I was honoured to be trusted with his emotions, but I'd never been told something so intimate. My friend group in real life consisted of two people, Kasey and Mani, and they were both closed off and kind of distant most of the time.

I didn't have the right words or reactions up against the clock, so we both left it there and didn't talk for a while. I messaged on the forums, but there was no-one to pick up the words. Did I fuck everything up? Was he grieving his brother or our friendship or both?

— — — —

— u/ Josh4265ab

Did I say something wrong?

-

— u/ Josh4265ab

I knew it was too early to talk in real life.

-

— u/ Josh4265ab

I'm here if you need me.

-

— u/ Josh4265ab

I know we haven't talked in a while, but do you ever feel like you're being watched and maybe your skin doesn't feel quite right, like it doesn't fit as snugly as before?

— — — —

2022

Leo re-entered my life in May. His message was a surprise, but it made sense. He'd been confused, hurt, angry, high, drunk, lost and a bunch of other things. He'd been to therapy and to the end of a bottle, but got through the main checklist of grieving. Anger. Pain. Sadness. Tick, tick,

tick. He didn't really have a friend group so the loss was even more profound, he said. I got it, but only kind of. I lost a dog when I was ten and couldn't explain the grief. This was more than that but maybe similar.

Our conversations became more and more regular. What started as a few scattered DMs became regular on-the-hour check-ins, and then a constant stream back and forth. Some people would have become overwhelmed. I just loved the company, the questions.

University came and went. I got a degree, a BA in Photography; maybe it would come in handy, but probably not. A random man in the forum offered me an internship but it seemed kinda shady and pornographic. I said thank you but no.

I got out and about and explored my city more. I took pictures of the sea and the beach. Portsmouth was a city of opposites, and I liked to explore that in my craft. Beautiful beaches and treacherous alleyways. Independent markets and soulless corporations on every street corner. I fed everything back to Leo and the forums, and we discussed the questions my work raised and how it was great that I was feeding my passion but maybe I should start finding paid work which made use of my degree.

I started taking headshots of local actors. Forehead forward, body slightly angled, try different characters and one smiling, one moody and one hot. I didn't have a studio but we had the Hilsea Lines and the boundless forest, which made a good backdrop, if a little cold and too natural. With the pandemic all but behind us, people were comfortable being out and about again (albeit at a distance), and I loved the process. It felt good to be creative, and even better to make some money out of it.

I made a bit of a name for myself and earned enough to

rent a small house. It wasn't comfortable but I had a roof over my head, a credit card, and a nice camera that allowed me to pay for weed and wifi, so what else did I really need?

Later that evening, I lit up a joint in the garden of some house party, surrounded by other local photographers who invited me along to network.

"What do you think our purpose as photographers is?" I asked between drags.

"I think we capture the beauty of the world through our own eyes," one person replied.

I hated that answer. I had to leave before I knocked the shit out of them.

Some random guy followed me from the party, said he loved my vibe and my outlook on the world or some shit. I asked him outright if he wanted to fuck me or if he was wasting my time; he said that he was actually looking to bum a cigarette, but maybe we could get intimate.

So we snuck into the woods and tasted each other's skin and felt what it was like to be inside of each other, until our faces scrunched up and nature took its course. Then we exchanged names and phone numbers, just in case we were up for something again. It was unlikely but I didn't want to be rude, so I added his details to my phone under *"Hookup 54"*. I don't know for sure that he was my 54th hookup, but I'd been with a lot of guys and the shape of the numbers looked good on my phone. Maybe I was just high.

I told Leo on the forums later that evening. He wasn't into fucking dudes as far as I knew, but he did love to examine and explore these random moments in time, so I didn't leave any detail unchecked. Not the guy's height or the size of his dick or the tears that spilled from his eyes when he finally shot his load. It all meant something, even if we couldn't decipher it.

— — — —

—— u/ LE02019xyk
Did he say anything once the whole thing was over?

-

— u/ Josh4265ab
I think he said he loved me and maybe wanted to spend his whole life with me? I was pretty high, so it was either that or nothing at all.

-

—— u/ LE02019xyk
People are weird right?

-

— u/ Josh4265ab
Yeah.

-

—— u/ LE02019xyk
What did he taste like?

— — — —

2023

These bits and pieces of conversations continued through our fifth year of friendship. We'd dropped the official anniversaries but often reminded each other that none of our relationships had lasted as long as this forum connection had. I sometimes wondered if that was sad or profound, but I couldn't quite come to a conclusion.

— — — —

— u/ Josh4265ab
We should mark five years in some way though, right?

Three dots bounced on screen. Leo was typing…
Thinking…

—— u/ LE02019xyk
We could meet in person?

I didn't expect that. I'd often been wary of ruining a good thing, and after the phone call debacle in 2021, wasn't it better to just exist within the forums? Friends and connections were a great thing when they blossomed naturally, but some connections existed in one space and not another. To start with, I felt that my friendship with Leo was just that: something amazing, but compartmentalised.

That's when he dropped the bombshell…

—— u/ LE02019xyk
I have to move. Is it weird of me to come to Portsmouth?

. . .

In a word, yes. It *was* a bit strange. But it was also everything I'd hoped for. When I thought about it, my real-world relationships had been just fine, fitting the space I gave them without intruding or spilling over, but it had been a long time since I felt really excited by a friend-ship or connection. Leo kept me on my toes, kept me fresh, kept me young. Having him around in real life would either be a dream come true or a true nightmare, but at this point in my life, I was ready to try something else.

I asked a half dozen questions and got a half dozen answers.

"Soon, I need a change of pace. Yes they know. No they don't know. Probably a flat or small apartment. No-one yet."

I picked apart his brain and started to form a real idea of him in my head. Off-screen, he was going to be a real, breathing presence in my life. I'd never been so scared or completely ecstatic. It was like an imaginary friend was coming to life. Most people didn't get that opportunity.

November 1st 2023.

The moving van arrived in front of the new flat. Random men moved furniture from the vehicle to the house, exchanging pleasantries with every passing motion, until it was strange and we made a silent agreement to just forget about polite small talk.

Leo arrived late, eventually rocking up at midday with sweat dripping from his forehead. He was tall, lean, and had messy but fresh shoulder-length hair. His face was handsome but unusual, like those peculiar model types you find in high fashion editorials.

He recounted his journey, what had gone right, what had gone wrong, and the multitude of characters he'd encountered on the ride. As he talked absolute shit, reeling off minute details about this and that, I remember feeling something in the pit of my stomach. This guy was a fool. An absolute joker. But he was also the most interesting person I think I'd ever met…

On the first night in the new flat, we ate packet ramen from mixing bowls, sat on frayed grey carpet and hand-me-down picnic blankets. We discussed life and politics and partners and the world at large, as if the forums had somehow materialised into a physical form. We'd take turns offering our words, receiving them, and deconstructing what they really meant.

Conversations were different with Leo. We didn't fill gaps with mindless utterances, talk over each other, or get bored of listening. There was an intent behind the whole thing. No gossiping, no shit talking, just analysis and emotion.

Time moved slowly that night. We shared a joint, took turns sucking up smoke and spilling embers, the cold air around us shifting in step with our breaths. My only other real friends, Kasey and Mani, texted to ask if they could see the new flat, but I made up an excuse about being tired and groggy and thought it was probably best if they just texted back tomorrow or the day after or maybe never.

I didn't feel comfortable with the idea of letting people into *this*. Those two were my best friends, my only other friends, but their idea of adult conversation spanned the very short space between who was hot in town and their latest conquests. I just couldn't envision a world in which they could co-exist with this new partnership. I was thinking too far ahead maybe, too deep in whatever this friendship was, but I couldn't risk it.

I don't know why Leo and I hadn't put up the new flat-pack beds before we inhaled so much weed, but we found each other holding A3 pamphlets at 1:00am, studying the animated characters and short instructions with exasperated sighs and screwed up eyebrows. These diagrams didn't make sense in the bright light of day whilst sober, let alone in this state, so we put in four screws and called it a night, returning to the picnic blankets and leftover ramen before passing out.

Present Day

We heard about the first disappearance on New Year's day. My uncle Bob's daughter, Kat (my cousin), was meant to be over at 12:00pm with bubble and squeak and trimmings, and when she didn't show up by 1:00pm, people started getting worried. Not only were they hungry, but as time ticked on and they were forced to eat crackers and whatever else was in the cupboard, they started to get that nervous bubbling in their stomachs. Bob's new wife Shelly made a whole drama about it, which didn't help, but she was a failed actress so it was the way she coped.

Kat didn't come home New Year's Day. People all but forgot about the feast they were promised when it got to 6:00pm and there was still no word from her.

As daylight fizzled into something black and abyss-like, there were rumours about disturbances at the beach.

CHAPTER 1

"It's weird that more people aren't talking about it."

Leo was laid across the bed, hair a mess, glow from his phone exposing his pale skin. His fingers tapped and scrolled, intermittently taking a break to dive into a bowl of peanuts. The crunching of nuts matched the pattern of his tapping. It was a weird thing to notice, but these patterns popped up every now and then, and I couldn't help but get sucked in by the accidental compositions.

"Right?"

I nodded, hoping he hadn't changed conversations when I drifted off.

"No reason for her not to turn up. Not to a family thing," I said.

Leo stretched, propping himself up on the bed. Something stole his attention on-screen. I could tell by the strange glint in his eyes.

"Look at this."

— — — —

F/ Portsmouth [latest]
u/ TODD88: *Missing Person - Katherine Jones* **21.**
Portsmouth resident. I'm her boyfriend, Todd. Things have been strange at home the last couple of days. It's something to do with our trip, I'm sure of it.

— — — —

"What trip did she go on?" Leo asked, cigarette poking from his lips, spilt ash peppered across his vest.

I didn't have many answers, because she and I weren't that close. The last time we spoke, it was about her new boyfriend, and that was a super-beige exchange. The girl had a way of speaking but not really saying much, her tongue wagging more of a workout than a way to communicate. As usual, I remembered her half-assed answers to my questions, but it was little more than filler.

"Todd. 28. No he's not too old. No I'm not too young. He's decent. Almost six inches. But he knows how to use it. Not yet. Probably. I probably should, but I'm on the pill. Don't worry."

Leo had already moved on, searching for more tidbits of information. The forums were a free-for-all, a vast abyss of text, categorised into sub-sections, but in a loose and often vague way.

"Did you try searching *Kat* and *Portsmouth* and *Missing Girl?*"

Leo looked up at me, aghast at such an obvious suggestion.

"No I thought I'd just put '*missing girl*' and see what spat up from ten years of posts. Idiot."

His tone was cheeky, I think. Blunt but playful. I was still learning his shades, his delivery, and how to differentiate his serious voice from his normal one. Five years of text-based messaging really left no room for nuance in real-life, and now all of these emotions and shit had become tangled into our conversations, it was very much a learning curve.

"I spoke to Uncle Bob. He and Shelly are beside themselves with worry."

Leo nodded. I was going to follow up my statement with something else, but I started thinking of semantics and how someone could be *beside themselves*.

I needed to smoke.

Phones down, we hung out on the balcony. Smoking time was our respite from technology.

"I didn't expect any of my family to go missing," I offered, hazy from my first toke, experiencing that strange blur of cold reality and daydream. "Especially not Kat. She's fucking boring. What would anyone want from her?"

Leo chuckled, the edges of his mouth curling inwards.

"Who did you think it would be, then?"

I pondered for a moment. That side of the family were boring. The most dramatic thing to come from that household was Bob's affair with Shelly when his first wife was on her deathbed. But then the wife found out and was kind of happy that he'd found someone else, and so everyone got on just great. I remember feeling like it could have been explosive. Top tier drama. Instead, it petered out, just like his first wife. Before we knew it, she was chucked in the fire, cremated, and put on the fireplace to watch over the new couple and Kat play happy families. Tragic.

There were some characters in my family. My Dad once stole ten beers from the local supermarket and had to pay a fine and do a half-day in jail. That was kind of cool. But it was also when he was a kid, before he got on the straight and narrow and became a policeman. That story was told every Christmas as a reminder that we all have flaws to overcome or some shit. I couldn't really connect because it was before my time and they didn't even have mobile phones back then.

"I honestly can't think."

Leo nodded. He wasn't disappointed. Just a natural break in conversation. My gaze lingered for a moment as I noticed the cold blue of his eyes stare back at me. I had to look up to break eye contact. On the roof opposite, a magpie was pecking the shit out of a pigeon carcass.

— — — —

We repeated our first-night tradition every Thursday. Picnic blankets on the floor in the living room. Ramen from mixing bowls. I wasn't really one for routines, but this felt right.

Leo was topless, leaning back on his elbows as he ate ramen and scrolled through his phone. The slurping was a bit annoying, but I didn't say anything.

"There's been an update to that Todd boy's post," Leo said, offering the screen.

— — — —

F/ Portsmouth [most recent]

Missing Person - Katherine Jones (UPDATE)

u/ TODD88:

It's me again. Todd. I had a missed call from Kat's phone. It was all robotic and shit. Kind of like those spam calls that take just a little too long to connect, and then it's about phone bills or whatever? Then it called back, two more times. Each time it was weirder. I can't describe it. Please let me know if you see her. This is a reminder of what she was wearing when she left:

Pastel pink dress. Flat black shoes. White socks with avocado pattern. Hair in a bun. Light makeup.

— — — —

I shook my head. I didn't really know what to think.

"It sounds like maybe she's just done a runner?"

Leo considered my sentence for a few moments, before shrugging it off. He slurped noodles from his chopsticks, catching beads of ramen juice with his tongue.

"Maybe."

CHAPTER 2

A great portion of this city was really fucking grey. Roads and structures and playgrounds and the skin of elderly people ambling around aimlessly. Through the windscreen, everything seemed distant and illusory, kind of like a film. I stared at every nook and cranny of the streets we wove through, Leo smoking in the passenger seat, exhaling years of his life in a grey fog.

I was looking for Kat, or someone with her shape and look at least, so the journey wouldn't feel entirely wasted and we could hold on to a tiny bit of hope. We started our journey in North End *(maximum grey)*, as it seemed like the kind of place a runaway would run away to. Then we slowly worked our way through Fratton *(medium grey)*, Southsea *(minimum grey)*, and then all the way back to Cosham *(somewhat grey)*.

We didn't find Kat, or anyone that had a similar look really. It wasn't a wasted journey. We stopped for ice cream and bought ingredients for dinner.

And then, on a long, winding track back to our house, a strange sight on the side of the street. Enough to make us pull up, park, and drag ourselves out into the bitter air just to get a closer look. It was flesh, for sure, blotches of pinky-white between red. There were no feathers or fur, which suggested it was closer to human than wild animal, but no confirmations either way.

Ew was my first thought. Then I tried to picture how it would taste cut up into our pasta dinner that evening. Probably an intrusive thought better kept to myself.

Leo wandered off, eyes tracking the landscape like they did his phone screen when he was in information-absorbing mode. The boy loved to learn, pick things apart, study their pieces. From one side to another, he tracked blood trails and scattered leaves and the way the grass settled from soft footprints.

It was really frustrating to me that flesh didn't have more of a context. If you were to see cubes of flesh lined up in a row, there would be no way to tell what it was from or even which part of the body. That was a flaw in natural design.

"What colour dress was she wearing?" Leo called out.

"Pastel pink according to boyfriend Todd."

Leo held up tattered shreds of a thin, pink, silky material. It was bloodstained and scorched. Definitely from a dress. I looked back at the flesh. Now I had a little context, there was a *slight* suggestion of it being human skin, though I couldn't place my finger on what properties gave it away.

As well as being repulsed, I was a little proud, too. This was the most interesting thing Kat had ever done, or ever been. A pile of flesh was more captivating than the twenty-one years of her life prior. That was a bit sad, but again, pretty poetic.

I scrolled my phone until Dad's name appeared. I

clicked, waited, and talked. I told him where we were, what we found, and that it might be time to schedule an awkward chat with Uncle Bob.

CHAPTER 3

Uncle Bob cried on the phone, first a little, then a lot. Officially, we had to wait for forensics and testing, but with the dress and a newly bought necklace we found as evidence, my dad thought it better to unofficially get to the point. Plus, Kat had a really shit tattoo of a rhino on her foot. Guess what was still visible on the dead flesh when we took a closer look?

That was one of my Dad's good qualities. He didn't fuck around. He got to the point.

Sometimes, I felt like it was a quality I lacked. My brain worked on tangents and deep dives, but it didn't hurt to keep it short sometimes. I thought about it a bit, but then returned to focusing on the strange colour that flesh turns when it's been hacked away from its source.

Shelly had turned up, against the advice of my Dad and the police. She broke down physically but her eyes just seemed to exude pure relief: at last there was no flesh connection between Bob and his ex-wife, and she could neatly slot into his life without the reminder of his past to dim her light. Aside from the ex-wife on the mantelpiece, but that'd be an easy fix in time—hide her in the loft.

The whole thing was mysterious, but also pretty damn tiring, so Leo and I retired to our house and ate pasta with red sauce. A sprinkling of parmesan and a heavy dose of conversation, and then we were so full we couldn't move, so just scrolled through our phones waiting for the news to hit the forums. When it did, it made the 'most popular' section for about twenty-three minutes.

— — — —

F/ Portsmouth [most popular]

u/ TODD88: Missing Person - Katherine Jones (UPDATE 2)

I can't believe it. We just had a call from the police. I feel empty. Sick. Disgusted. WHO DOES THIS TO A PERSON???? We thought it might be an animal but there aren't enough remains to tell. There will be an investigation, and if I find out who's done this to my precious girlfriend. Well, I can't say on here what I'd do BUT IT WILL BE FUCKING BAD. CUNTS!!!

F/ SuicideWatch [most popular]

u/ TODD88: Just had bad news. Need drugs. Or just death.

As per title. Can't carry on. Fuck this place. Fuck Portsmouth. Full of cunts. Anyone got weed or heavier?

— — — —

Leo passed out on the sofa. He looked full and happy. I watched some TV, scrolled, and thought about sneaking off for a wank but had a weird feeling about masturbating in a house with a stranger, which technically he still was. I decided to leave it for twenty minutes and see if the moment passed, but every time I looked over at Leo, I felt that maybe he was quite attractive and I'd quite like to kiss him on the forehead and tuck him in. Whatever. It was all emotions and where had they ever got anyone?

After another ten minutes of shitty cop TV, I snuck to the bathroom and slung my jeans around my ankles, beat my meat whilst visualising a dirty amalgam of flesh and blood and body parts and maybe Leo's face was in there too, I can't remember. I squirted my load into the bowl and onto the toilet seat, which I mopped up with folded tissue paper. Leo knocked the bathroom door moments later, asking if I'd seen the latest posts. I told him I'd be out in a minute and cleaned everything one more time to make sure the stickiness was gone.

"We have to investigate this."

I stared at him for a few moments, deciphering the urgency in his gaze.

"The police are investigating it. I told you, my Dad's part of it."

"That's not what I mean. You saw the flesh, right?"

I nodded. I had. The putrid scent was still lingering between the crusty contents of my nostrils.

"That wasn't just a random killing. Especially not an animal. Something weird is going on."

We were interrupted by something outside. The sky outside lit up momentarily, a flash of warm yellow cascading across our windows.

"Is that lightning?" I asked. We both walked over to the window.

"I hope it clears up before tomorrow," he muttered.

I completely forgot I'd promised him a camping trip. I'd argued that outdoor adventures were probably best left to the Summer—and when random people weren't being killed across the city—but he'd persisted and countered that maybe some fresh air would do us both good. I still don't know why I agreed so easily.

CHAPTER 4

The idea of sleeping in a tent filled me with dread. But still, I found myself in the driver's seat traversing winding roads and a long bridge out of the city, on our way to the campsite on Hayling Island.

The island was largely a tourist destination, boasting a small theme park, plenty of pristine coastline and countryside, and events of all descriptions. In the summer, it was an absolute nightmare to get to and from—the one bridge leading to the mainland was always rammed—but in the gloomy mid-week Autumn, it was pretty much dead.

I tried to bargain with Leo: a caravan or something other than a fabric tent would be much more comfortable for us both to share. He rejected that outright, and said the idea wasn't to be comfortable, but to have an experience. An experience of getting a cold and spending the rest of the week coughing and sneezing, perhaps, but I didn't fight it. Something told me it was futile to argue with him.

Under a light drizzle and the silver blanket of clouds above, the campsite looked exactly as you'd expect a

British 'holiday' to look: crowds of rowdy teens, off-brand beer, dirty caravans, half-pitched tents, and middle-aged men walking around in shorts and flip flops. Leo sparked right into action, ambled to our pitch and marked the perimeter for the tent. I inhaled, then exhaled with a silent sigh, and started to help.

As night fell, a random couple over the field invited us to eat BBQ with them. The air was heavy with oppressive clouds and static energy, intermittent rain sweeping across the site. Occasional bolts of lightning lit up the sky, over-powering the tiny fire we'd set in the middle. I looked to Leo. He ate the BBQ burger meticulously, chiseling away the food in neat bites whilst paying just the right amount of eye contact to our hosts, the couple.

Bev and Simon weren't *our* kind of people, per se. They talked about where they came from *(Portsmouth)*, why they were there *(just got engaged—I congratulated them twice)* and how long they'd be spending at the site *(just the two nights, as Bev needed to get back to her care work job)*. It was the kind of information that just took up space in the brain, but I gladly received it in return for some hot dogs and burgers. And I'd gladly shit out every word they'd said along with my waste in the grimy portaloo tomorrow morning.

In some ways, I was happy not to share any of our deep conversations with these people who, as lovely as they were, weren't meaningful in our lives beyond the scope of this trip. The small talk was transactional, polite, *British.* But after saying our goodbyes, adding each other on Facebook and retiring to our separate accommodation (if you could call a piece of fabric on a pole such a thing), a wave of relief washed over me.

Leo stripped his shirt off and snuggled deep into a sleeping bag. I switched on a small battery-powered lamp, which cast a cosy orange glow around the space. I listened to the wind and the rain and the remnants of gossip and screams from children who were just as thrilled to be out in the wet weather as I was.

I checked the messages on my phone. A string of consolations and 'sorries' about Kat, which felt kind of surreal and uninvited. I kept trying to get people to understand we really didn't know each other well. There was also spam, and more shit from the family. Maybe it was good to take a break from the screen.

"You good?" Leo asked. I nodded.

"Yeah. You?"

He returned the gesture.

"I bought a joint, if you want to—?"

"Oh God, yes."

We slunk off to the side of the beach, gently crunching the pebbles underfoot as we attempted to blend in with the shadows. Rumbling waves echoed, omnipresent eyes watching from afar. Maybe campsite workers, maybe God. Either way, we didn't want to get caught.

The first hit of weed was great. The second was too, but a bit less. I wondered why I smoked so much weed? Why was it always something I felt like telling people I do? Because my life kinda sucked, I guess.

I'm pretty certain we talked about something amazing and important and possibly philosophical, but all that melted away when Leo suggested we jump in the water. Skinny dipping, in the cold depths of Autumn...

"I don't think so. I didn't bring a towel."

"We'll heat up in the car. Dry off with our dirty clothes."

A million excuses spilled from my mouth. Leo had a million and one comebacks. I lost again.

As I unzipped my jeans, trying to keep every last ounce of warmth in my upper body until the last moment, I found myself frozen in spirit, as opposed to temperature. The moonlight lit up Leo's body in ethereal chiaroscuro, patches of light and shadow, an enigmatic form ripped straight from a painting or my dreams or something.

I'd never really felt anything that crossed the platonic line towards this boy. The line was so firmly drawn in the sand, it could have been decked out with mines and traps. I wouldn't have dared consider anything more than friendship, let alone act on any feeling. Once or twice, I thought he looked cute and maybe I'd want to kiss him in a protective, nurturing way, to remind him that I cared. But this was something else. A few seconds of movement, of his skin reflecting the refractions of water and light, and our whole friendship was under the lens.

"What you staring at?" Leo fired.

I shook my head. He laughed, taking it in his stride. He was already topless with his belt in his hand. I was trailing behind.

Staring at the floor, I finished unzipping my jeans and pulled them to the floor, stepping out of each leg.

"You don't have to stop."

"What?" I asked.

"Staring, I mean… I'm not hiding anything."

What the fuck did that mean? The splashing of the waves intensified as I grabbed at the bottom hem of my shirt.

But as the shadows in front of me came to life and transitioned into a moving silhouette, I stopped in place. Leo noticed my apprehension, turned to look towards the sea, and recoiled at the sight.

Just metres away, clouded by the gentle abyss behind

it, a human-like form stood half-submerged. With water sluicing from it, and an unsteady gait, the form revealed itself to be possibly male, but it was too dark to tell.

Stepping into the light, the mystery evaporated. It was someone in a yellow, rubber hazmat suit, with torn, crimson shreds ripped through the legs and chest.

"Hello? Do you need help?"

They didn't reply. Just thrashed. Waved. Exploded into a frantic display of arm gestures. Urged us to retreat.

"Get away!" Grunting and fighting through the water, they brushed free of the waves. Standing on the shore, they pointed their arm back up towards the campsite. "GO!" he screamed, a distorted male voice crackling through the mask.

Didn't need to tell us twice…

Leo was already in motion. Blades of the sharp grass unique to the British shoreline swiped our ankles as we hastily retraced our steps back to the campsite. We didn't dare turn backwards, in case the stranger was right behind us. There was no context to the situation: what had we just walked in on? Something we shouldn't have, that's for sure.

In the tent, we zipped all sides, our skin dripping from sweat. I counted my breaths, Leo squeezed his eyes shut. The air was thick. Panic engulfed us both.

Then we burst into laughter, a weird, inexplicable joy that felt warm and orange like the glow from the battery lamp. It unfroze us, we returned to the evening and the present moment.

"That was *fucked!*" he gleamed.

"Do we call the police? I'm fucking shaking."

Leo shook his head.

"Let's not get involved in that shit. I'm too fucking stoned. We can tell your Dad in the morning."

Our bodies were cold, but once wrapped into our separate fabric cocoons, we inched towards each other to share warmth. Though cushioned orange material separated our skin, we breathed in step, inhaling and exhaling like a single lifeform. I don't think I'd been this close to anyone ever.

— — — —

The next morning burned through the unconscious dark, whilst my dreams transitioned to reality. Leo was up, probably eating or pissing, but I was shaped like a semicircle, contorted across the floor cover like a worm. I stretched out into something more human, then bent forward into a sitting position. I'd slept as well as could be expected, but I was in the middle of a fucking field, so I didn't feel well-rested or particularly ready to start my morning.

The surreal liminality of campsite convenience shops is impossible to describe to anyone who hasn't experienced a British camping trip. I reflected on this as I rifled through the strange, all-beige space.

I wanted two things: crisps and answers. I could get the former from here, and the latter from someone who worked on site. But probably not the sixteen-year-old clerk scrunched behind a makeshift desk, hooked to their phone. I grabbed two multipacks and a small chocolate bar, pulled out my card, was given an apathetic spiel about it being cash only, and left with just one multipack and no coins left in my wallet. The air was wet, and something was up.

On the field, crowded near the manky toilet block, a small group had gathered around something on the floor. I opened the pack and pulled out a smaller, individual bag of salt and vinegar. Tore the seam, stuck one on my tongue, dissolved the tang. Chewed it up and looked closer at the ground.

An old man, seventy or eighty or something more elderly, was contorted into a tight ball, hands in front of his face, as if cowering or begging someone not to hurt him. His flesh looked blue, smelt sour, and was caked in some kind of yellow fuzz. On closer inspection (after moving some nosy child to the left, hide your eyes pal) the fuzz was mossy. Fungal. It looked as if it had been painted on… No, that was too neat. Maybe like squirted with whip cream or silly string. Textural and fluffy. It spread right from his neck into his mouth and in there it was cavernous and dead. The ground around him was wet with blood. The downtrodden green had turned more of a rust-brown.

I shook crumbs into my mouth, scrunched the packet into my jacket pocket.

"You got any prawn cocktail?"

Leo arrived, nodding at the body.

"I've been here about ten minutes. No police yet," he said.

"Jesus."

I was rifling through the multipack bag subconsciously. Then I kicked myself, remembering.

"They discontinued prawn cocktail. Ready salted okay?"

Leo sighed but agreed, crunching moments later.

For a moment, I wondered if this was the man we'd

seen last night, having caught his death splashing out at sea at his age. But he was too old. His eyes too sunken in. A few inches shorter and wider probably, maybe more. And no hazmat suit to be seen...

The sound of Leo chewing annoyed me slightly. I think my chewing did the same for him. But we didn't say anything. When it was time to go and the hi-vis jackets danced into a cordon, I noticed some of the man's skin was detached. Not neatly. More like *gored*. Ripped away. That couldn't have been a comfortable way to go. It definitely made me uncomfortable.

For some reason, we were hungry again as soon as we left. Off the island and back in the city, we went to a place called Portsdown Hill. It used to be famous for war memorabilia and walking routes, but now it was known mostly for the burger van.

Two coffees, two monster burgers with egg and sausage (but not bacon, as it looked too much like detached skin), and some kind of cookie each. We sat in my car overlooking the city as I chomped down, yolk splashing onto my beard. I wiped it away with a scratchy napkin, coagulated remnants already dried-in.

"My brother had the same look in his eyes when he died," Leo mentioned, referring back to the old man's corpse. I wasn't quite sure how to respond.

"I'm sorry about that," I tried, and I knew that Leo appreciated the effort.

My mind wasn't focused on the old man's loose flesh or even the way he had been so tight and twisted. No, the fungus was the problem for me. This dude was *riddled* in it, and the idea of it growing inside his mouth and gums and cheeks grossed me out a lot, so much so that I had to pause eating and burn away the sensation with black coffee.

Leo looked at me.

"You're thinking about the fungus too, right?"

He stopped eating and we both downed our coffees together, praying away the shared mental sensation of fluffy yellow.

CHAPTER 5

Leo had an interview at the arcade by the beach. He'd applied for several minimum wage roles before moving, but no-one had got in touch until recently. There were worse places to work than the arcade.

I thought it would be as good a time as any to pull out some 35mm and take a few moody monochrome shots. He stepped inside the apathetic circus of bright lights, old video games, and funfair tat, and I headed to the pebbles. I'd already loaded some 400 speed film (perfect for overcast days) and let my mind discover a composition. There weren't many people around, just a few stragglers and litter pickers. Boats drifted past, a big ferry made an appearance, but nothing called out to me. My old tutor argued that there was no such thing as inspiration, and that one could spend their whole life looking for it and be no further along when they died of old age.

I didn't want that to be me, so subconsciously I said *fuck it* and lined up the horizon, taking a shot right out to sea. In the bottom right of my viewfinder, distorted by the cylindrical angle, some kind of van was parked up just out of the way. I clicked the shutter and snapped the moment, then turned my attention to the vehicle.

It wasn't weird to see vans parked up here—they were usually just tradespeople or whatever—but this looked really out of place. The van had chrome plated panels, anachronistic details, and a big fuck off coil of orange hosepipe at the back, which was fully extended beyond my field of vision.

Someone's trying to steal the water, I imagined for just a second, then inwardly cursed at myself for such a stupid thought. My brain was jelly at times.

I lined up the composition, thought it was more interesting than the sea on its own, and tried to take a snap. But a weird light kept dazzling the lens and, try as I might, I couldn't find the source. Unless a second sun had risen and changed the laws of the universe as we knew them, there was no way such a bright light could flank both sides. A strange groaning sound also erupted from nearby, but I couldn't place that either.

When I lowered the camera, two men in yellow plastic hazmats recoiled the hose and hopped into the front of the van. They sped back toward the road, and as I tried to take a shot one more time, the passenger angled a mirror on the inside, completely burning my field of view. Eyes sealed tight, I depressed the shutter and rewound, firing off three shots before it felt comfortable to open my eyes again.

When my eyes opened, a man screamed at me from under a tree. He was in an awkward position, jeans slung around his ankles. It took me a moment to realise his lower body was entangled in some girl's, his cock deep in her. I guess that's what the groaning sound was.

"Oh, no, I'm not—"

He shook his head. Must have thought I was a right pervert.

"Not for free, anyway!" I joked, immediately feeling like an absolute bell-end. At least he laughed at the joke.

"I thought you were photographing the sea, weirdo."

Leo was back, and had seen the whole thing.

"I was trying to capture—"

"Whatever. Let's get back and develop them, I missed half the action."

We ambled back to the car, in no particular rush nor delay.

"I really was just taking pictures of the sea," I explained.

"Whatever you say."

A moment of awkward silence.

"How was the interview?" I asked.

"All good. I probably got it. The uniforms look itchy. But the girl was hot, so there's that."

I nodded. I imagined the uniform and the girl who might have conducted the interview. In my mind, she had light brunette hair and ample tits and maybe a cute red lipstick. She'd flirt with Leo and discuss their hobbies outside of work, then reach under the table and stroke his leg with a poisonous look in her eyes.

It didn't take long until my daydream relocated Leo and the imaginary girl back at the tree we'd just left. In my mind, Leo was completely naked and thrusting into the imaginary girl so hard she was being pushed across the grass whilst her pussy leaked, unable to control her quivering.

"We're going the wrong way," Leo muttered, eating the last bag of crisps from the multipack. He shook the crumbs into his gaping mouth. I didn't need to make any more sexual connections, so I focused on the road whilst he no doubt focused on what he'd say to get that girl into bed.

Lucky bitch.

— — — —

F/ Portsmouth [latest]
u/ RosePetalSummer: Shoplifters. WTF?!

It's no secret we have loads of thieves in this area, but fuck me, does my shop have an open invitation on it? Group of two or three, faces all fucked up with acne and blisters, came in, trashed the place and just took some gum. What is the reason for that? Why won't the police do anything? I need to move and honestly venting has helped a lot.

-

—> u/ AshleyMadson3

It happened to my shop too. I'm a florist. Make it make sense!?

-

— —> u/ Rorytalks

And me. Cooking shop. They took knives. I guess that makes sense at least?

-

—> u/ AshleyMadson3

Still not good though is it?

-

— — —> u/ ae445yy2hh3h

Fuckers. Don't need know why. Supplies ain't cheap. Look up once in a while, more to life. Fidgeting itchy and no brain, got no idea about any of this shit. Shut yourself. Or maybe open. Open up. Learn somethin. Accept.

\-

u/ RosePetalSummer

Does anyone else know what the fuck any of that means?

CHAPTER 6

Vibrant red. More red than you've ever seen in your life. We'd fashioned a darkroom out of our closet, and my mind immediately recalled the camping shop and what a weird space it was, and how weird the man and his dead furry face—

— *Nope.*

Not doing that.

The film reel was in a cylindrical tank with some developer. In a kind of hypnotic pattern, I rocked it back and forth, agitating the mixture.

Half a dozen boring processes (and plenty of coffee) later, I had the developed film, and it was practically all useless. Squinting at the negatives, I could see bright flashes of light and my first half-decent picture of the sea. Everything else was a waste of time. I didn't get any usable snaps of the enigmatic van people. It was all unfocused and blurry.

I told Leo and he was more empathetic than I expected.

"I want answers. It's all too fucking weird," I complained, and then followed it up with an "oh well" because my self-help audiobook said I shouldn't complain so much.

"Why don't we document it, I mean properly?"

I tilted my head like an interested dog, inviting more information.

"Look, I have a part-time job now, you'll get some photo gigs soon. But instead of smoking away every spare minute, why don't we start taking some footage, maybe put it online? There's obviously something happening there."

"Like a documentary?" I asked.

Leo was feverish, excited.

"Exactly. We both love a mystery: we can hype people up on the forums. Let's do some investigating."

I agreed. A week later, we were back at the beach, armed with some amateur equipment and a rudimentary understanding of filmmaking techniques.

We had a bit of back and forth about structure and intent, and decided it made sense for Leo to be on camera, a character our audience could relate with. I'd do the camera and mic and we'd edit together.

Our first shots were clumsy, out of focus, god-awful sound. Leo had to learn how to behave in front of a camera, which always seemed easy in theory but not when your innermost worries and flaws were magnified times a hundred or maybe a thousand. But he picked up his groove, started treating the camera like a friend, and I thought that we might be onto something.

The first good shot I got was down by the shore, where a dozen gored, decapitated fish were flopped and strewn around the area. It was a horrifying scene, almost night-marish in scale and brutality. Torn flesh and cherry innards made patterns between pebbles of all descriptions.

In addition to all that, the fish were full of greenish foam and a coating of yellow fungal spores. I panned across the scene, gently gliding side to side to ensure the footage was smooth. If people really wanted to get a sense of the pure filth laid out in front of them, they'd have that opportunity from this visual.

Leo put on his most professional presenter persona, and crouched down right beside the seaside massacre.

"In the latest of a series of weird events in Portsmouth, these headless…"

Leo stared at them for a second.

"Fish—I don't know what kind they are—but anyway, they're full of fungus and some disgusting liquid."

"Don't touch anything," I warned him. He continued talking into camera, and thankfully didn't pick up any of the diseased creatures.

The next day, we sat on the floor in our living room whilst cutting together the first batch of footage. We wouldn't be winning a prize any time soon, not for journalism nor camerawork, but it was definitely usable.

Leo's eyes scrunched up when he focused. Battling the glow of the bright white screen, his pupils grew and shrunk depending on the exposure of the shot, his hair slicked back behind his ears.

"You're a natural at this," I said, watching over his shoulder as he carefully snipped and trimmed the shots.

"We're a dream team, man," he replied, a smirk growing on his face.

The bubble of the moment burst with a deep thud and clatter outside the window. I quickly hopped up and over to the balcony, looking over the edge. A tall, skinny guy, with longish hair and unsteady gait, was smashing his hand against the door.

"What the fuck is going on?" I shouted down.

My words weren't connecting. The guy was in his own world, daydreaming or nightmaring or something in between. His body was arched, bones prominent through his dirty, puke-stained t-shirt. I couldn't make out many details at all, just scraggly hair bulging out underneath a soiled grey beanie, and ripped jeans. Stumbling back and forth in the same square foot of space, his rickety posture slowly buckled with each blow against the front door.

Leo appeared behind me.

"What's going on?"

"It's some drunk guy, I think."

"That's wild. It's not even 2:00pm on a Thursday. You want some lunch?"

CHAPTER 7

Due to our increasingly frequent proximity, Leo and I didn't really share messages with each other on the forums now, which was kind of sad but obvious. Instead, we had a habit of logging on to our own respective devices, and jumping into conversations that lit a spark in us. We'd talk about the different things we found, sometimes cross paths on the same posts, team up on any trolls who were talking shit.

— — — —

F/ Portsmouth [latest]
u/ JayABw: What's going on at the beach?
Me and my girlfriend usually go for a walk around 7pm, down Palmerston Road through to Clarence Esplanade, get some ice cream and then come back. Last night, we decided to walk close to the water, and there were just dead fish everywhere.

Also, a couple of weird fucking guys were hanging around us, telling us to wait and watch the sky and see 'them'.

Where do I get the same drugs as these crackheads?

— — — —

"We should release our doc," Leo said without hesitation.

"Like now?"

"People are already talking about the fish. I think it's time we get into the conversation properly."

It was as good a time as any, but part of me grew concerned at giving up my anonymity. The forums had always been a safe place for secret discussions and hiding behind the keyboard, but I guess we were getting older, and this comfort zone would have to be challenged eventually. The documentary was only four minutes long—it was more of a teaser than anything else—but it was definitely interesting enough to get people's attention. It was the first part of something bigger, something that was intangible for now but would become clearer each time we shot something new.

So Leo exported the video with a creepy soundtrack, a basic colour grade, and some fuck-ugly but kind of ironic title fonts.

— — — —

F/ Portsmouth [latest]
  u/ JayABw: What's going on at the beach?

—> u/ *LE02019xyk*

Me and [Josh4265ab] went down and filmed some things earlier today. Check this shit out.

LINK: *www.gofetchvid.com/southseafishcapade*

— — — —

And then it was up. All of it. Our hard work, new hobby, identities and friendship, out on the web for people to watch and enjoy and critique and slam. Who knew what ratio those reactions would take, but it felt good to be putting something out there, despite my reservations.

As the likes and comments filtered through across the evening, I could see Leo grow more and more ecstatic, and it rubbed off. I had one of those moments where you feel yourself in the present and suddenly realise everything around you is real and you're breathing and everything is actually happening right fucking now.

Leo suddenly turned to me with a giant smile on his face. His eyes were relieved, excited, restless.

"This is so cool!"

He rolled onto his knees and pulled me into a big embrace, before flopping right on top of me. I fell with the momentum, ending up on my back, pinned down by his lanky frame. His hair dangled onto my face, tickling, teasing. His eyes were focused on me, and just me, his warm breath stirring across my skin. A few moments seemed like a lifetime, and I was completely mesmerised and confused and stunned.

Then he pulled me up, returned to his seated position,

and reeled off some of the comments, his own face reflecting my mixed emotional state.

"Listen to what they're saying… *'This is so fucking weird, please make more…', 'These guys need to make more videos…'* I think the consensus is clear, Josh," he said.

As he finished his sentence, the lights flickered with a low buzz. Screams ripped into our interior world from outside—the guy from before was back slamming on the door, spewing nonsense. Fuzzy static erupted on the TV; the computer screen glitched like a wet appliance. An unholy shriek tore through the flat, followed by a resounding, guttural echo. A window shattered in the kitchen. The late evening sky cracked to reveal devastating bolts of lightning outside. We both jumped to our feet. Leo reached for the camera from the table, and began recording.

Against any kind of common sense, we filed out onto the small balcony, and stood in awe as a strange opaque shape flickered in the sky in the distance, ripples of something caressing the atmosphere around it. An abrupt jolt of tungsten orange, and then things were calm again. Steady. Back to normal.

We looked at each other for a moment. Sweat rolled down my forehead, dampened my armpits. In the distance, chatter filled the humid air. Down by our front door, crimson streaks of blood and pulp were spread across the road like a broken jar of jam.

A putrid scent hung at head height, wafting in our face as we both stepped out on the street apprehensively. Piles of savagely burned, rotten meat were slopped at random points on the tarmac. A group of local residents had popped their heads out the door to find the source of the disturbance. Most of them recoiled at the sight of fresh blood, but all I could think about was how this was the first time I'd ever seen my immediate neighbours. Weird.

"I don't want to go any closer."

Leo lowered the camera. His face was screwed up, sickly and apprehensive. He couldn't tear his eyes away from the carnage. I walked back, slung an arm around him, and guided him back inside.

He vomited twice before we got to his room.

— — — —

F/ Portsmouth [latest]
u/omenoftheyoung: Theories about the sound earlier.

You all heard it. People are saying it's Russia or China, but that thing didn't look military. I used to be in the Army. Friends across the forces. This was something else. What are they hiding?

-

—> u/ jonnyboi

So what do you think it is?

-

u/ Omenoftheyoung:

Dunno. Something weird. Aliens? Wouldn't surprise me at this point.

-

——> u/ hookupsinpompey

Anyone got coke? I'll pay top price. DM me.

CHAPTER 8

Leo was weird after the incident, a grey cloud stalking the flat. I'd never seen him like this. He was so curious when we discovered Kat's flesh (RIP) and had basically sprinted *towards* the freaky fish disaster. I guess this was different, and maybe he wasn't as desensitised as me, but I found that hard to believe. He's the one who showed me all those violent deaths on that website years ago. The name escapes me, but it was definitely all fucking disgusting. We bonded over how we felt, and now it all felt a bit pointless.

The next morning, I helped him gather his things for day one at the arcade job. He had breakfast and told me he was looking forward to playing games on his break and meeting his colleagues, but something had him in a funk. I'd talk to him about it later.

I dropped him off and took the long way home to clear my head. I had three missed calls in the span of ten minutes and realised I'd promised my dad I'd meet him for brunch on the hill.

It was too early for monster burgers but it was also too early to discuss such heavy family issues, so I said fuck it and got an egg and bacon (because I was almost over the weird detached flesh and the look on that old man's dead face).

And then I listened as my father reeled off information about Kat's investigation and his other work in apathetic monotone. We discussed deaths and assaults and shady government contracts all between bites of oily sandwich. We had a lot of trouble connecting, had done our whole life, but with him as my only parent, and me as his only child, I felt a sense of duty. It wasn't all bad. I got to satisfy my morbid curiosity and get all of the gossip, and he basically paid for everything I ate and half my rent.

"How's Leo? Is he all settled in?"

I nodded, wiping my mouth with my sleeve.

"He's got his first day at the arcade. But he's kinda bummed out."

"How come?"

"We saw a dead body last night."

My Dad recoiled. Maybe I *was* too desensitised.

"What do you mean?"

I shrugged.

"Just that. Dead body. Outside the flat."

"I was in Winchester all night. Why didn't I hear about this? I don't remember any call-ins, not from your area."

I shrugged, took another bite—the bacon was feeling weird again. I hope I wasn't going to be put off it by all this death.

"There was blood and bits everywhere. He definitely didn't survive. Unless people's flesh can just magic back together."

Dad shook his head. Not answering the question, just in disbelief.

"Maybe the rain washed him away? It got really heavy that night," I offered as a potential explanation.

This time my Dad shrugged.

"Maybe. We'll check the sewers."

I could only imagine what you'd find looking down there.

— — — —

Dad dropped me back home and I planned to develop some more 35mm. I had a roll from the video shoot that I hadn't even thought about in a few days, and there might be some magic shots in there. I had all the good intentions but then I got a text from Leo which bummed me out enough to send me off to bed for a nap.

"You cool if I invite Cara from work over? Could be an extra pair of hands on the video…"

The girl who interviewed him. I knew something like this would happen.

Peeking out from underneath my blanket, I let the cool air from the cracked window caress my face. But after a few minutes, it felt spiky and uncomfortable, so I completely hid underneath it. I slept for half hour or a little more, my mind racing at the idea of letting some random girl join us.

Around 3:00pm, I got up, showered and charged the equipment. We'd invested in a little on-camera LED light so we could shoot at night. There were murmurs on the forums about weird meet-ups by the beach and blood and condoms being found on the pier in the early hours, so at the very least, it would be a starting point. I'd be doing all the technical stuff, Leo could use his on-screen charm, and Cara could go and buy coffee or hold the mic or something. We'd work it out.

The plan was to try and find some kind of connection between all the weird puzzle pieces of information we'd encountered the last week or so. Kat's body, the old man, the hazmat at the sea. There was a connection, I was sure.

— — — —

F/ Portsmouth [latest]
u/ rascallion89: You're wasting your time.

We're all sitting here getting butt-fucked by government and hating each other and having no money to live and fucking dying in our own homes but sure let's just all keep arguing and gossiping and shit. We're too comfortable. In this flesh. Have you ever just imagined ripping it away and walking around truly naked, completely vulnerable to the world? I have. I'm considering it. I'll give them my skin and be truly free. Who's joining me?

EDIT:

It's cold. dark. Fuckingg lights, what is it?

CHAPTER 9

I'd imagined the girl that interviewed Leo would be brunette with massive tits and red lips. That image was completely obliterated when the real girl stood in front of me: skinny, kind of goth vibes—if goth still meant anything—and an oozing sense of melancholy and dread. She was nice enough, tried to shake my hand (which was weird and led to an even more awkward hug), but I figured she'd probably hold the mic and keep out of things which made me happier. Leo kept glaring at her, which felt strange to me, but was probably endearing.

"Leo's said a lot about you."

"Hasn't he worked there like one shift?" I asked, before feeling like a dick and following it up with, "that means he hasn't got to the bad bits yet."

She chuckled. Leo relaxed. I sighed with relief.

At the beach, the sun was dipping, golden streaks cutting through the grey. The only people out were dog-walkers and tourists, so we took a moment to get coffee and think things through. Hopefully, something more interesting would appear, otherwise we'd have to make up something dramatic and engaging. We had fans, Leo and I, and I didn't want us to fuck that up. Not due to lack of content or some work fling or my red-hot feelings about the situation.

I set up my tripod in the last moments of daylight and attached the camera and LED. Leo looked dazzled and malnourished under the intense light, so I cranked it down thirty percent and brought the life back into his face. Cara asked lots of questions about holding the mic, so I reeled off the basics and assured her she'd do fine. I'd set up the camera to record from the internal mic anyway, so nothing she did or didn't do really mattered.

I gestured 3,2,1 with my fingers and Leo started to talk, bringing some energy to the drab setting.

"We've been hearing rumours about strange findings near South Parade Pier, so have set up base to see what we can find."

His voice sounded weird in my headphones, so I relented and switched the audio to external mic and got him to repeat the line. Cara was holding the mic perfectly, the audio was crystal clear. Bitch.

After repeating the sentence word for word, a young, kind of chubby guy popped into the background, right next to the water. His skin was glistening, as if he'd already spent plenty of time amongst the salty waves. I think I recognised him from university, but the whole city was full of students. His eyes were rolling all over the place, a series of deep gashes torn into his side. Leo and I shared a look, and nodded.

After a silent decision, we started walking over. Cara trailed behind with the mic cable. I let the tripod rest on the pebbles, and Leo joined the mysterious stranger.

"Are you okay mate? It's too cold for swimming trunks. And you look hurt."

The boy stared at him, and then the camera. I noticed a peppering of strange yellow pits in his face. His eyes were kind of milky, a light but sour hue.

"They're late. I'm here. They'll be…"

His neck snapped to look up at the sky, then his head fell forward to expel a flurry of orange vomit. There were far too many solid chunks for that to be healthy. Even under the dying light of sunset, it was easy to tell he was super sick.

"Soon. I think."

Without warning, the boy dug a soiled finger into an abscess in his chest, exploring the sticky wet opening with a jagged nail. His mouth drooped euphorically whilst he was in there, until he pulled out, wiped away the sloppy gunge, and dove into the freezing sea.

The camera captured it all. We stayed another five minutes or so and then left, the image of the boy's self-mutilation hot in all our minds.

— — — —

Leo invited Cara back. I was bored of being standoffish so I made her a cup of tea. We didn't have food in, so takeout was on the cards, but in the end I settled for beans on toast.

Cable connected to the PC, I sat in the corner of the living room ingesting footage, whilst Leo and Cara talked a bit in his room. We hadn't spoken one-on-one all day, which was the longest time I'd gone without quality conversation in years. Sure, there'd been passing comments about the day and the weird boy with his sticky, self-harming finger, and how the city was basically going to shit at a faster rate than usual, but everything else had been painfully polite and bordering on small talk.

The footage was frustratingly slow to upload, so I opened the forums and tried to stimulate my mind.

— — — —

F/ Portsmouth [latest]

u/ beepityboopity: Some guy just attacked me at the beach. Worth calling police?

I was at South Parade walking my dog, and some teen jumped out of the water and hurled abuse at me. I ignored, but he followed me and pushed me down. Kicked my dog. We're both fine but a bit shook up. Worth talking to police?

—> u/ justjjan
Call 101 I think.

— — — —

Reading the post, I couldn't help but make the connection. I had to get involved.

— — — —

———> u/ Josh4265ab

Did this guy have freckles? Yellow acne, lots of gashes on his body?

-

u/ beepityboopity

Yeah. How did you know? Were you there. Could maybe do with a witness if I take it further…

-

———> u/ Josh4265ab

No. Was there earlier. Have some footage of him acting strange. Let me know if you need anything to help ID him.

-

u/ beepityboopity

Okay. Thanks, will do. All points to drugs if you ask me.

— — — —

I didn't ask him, but I got his gist.

The silence of the room felt heavy and unwelcome. Leo's room had gone quiet, aside from a soft, wet noise. They were kissing. I was sure of it.

Back to the footage. I watched as the files rendered, a slowly increasing percentage. I couldn't touch the edit until it was done. My fingers were tapping. Rubbing against one another anxiously. I was bored, frustrated, tired… Gentle laughter and light conversation oozed from the other room. I wished I was part of it. And then more squelchy sounds… Kissing? Fucking?

I hopped up silently and put my ear to the door to confirm it. Then my vision and mind went full-red, and I hopped back onto the forums. I was going back to old habits.

— — — —

F/ PortsmouthGayMeets
u/ Josh4265ab: Looking for casual.

Early 20's. Brown hair. Cute face. Skinny. Looking for casual, anything is fine by me. Can host. DM me.

— — — —

I don't think I even felt horny when I wrote it, but Leo had well and truly fucked me off and I needed to rage somehow.

There were a string of DM's in minutes:

— — — —

u/ ostrichpecker: *in portsmouth halls. wanna meet? 22 here.*

-

u/ dirtyjohnsfavbeard: *31. male. can't host but can travel. suck/fuck/ more?*

-

u/ bin23bread: *you ever fucked a guy with no legs?*

— — — —

I picked the second one down and hopped on chat, got his number and a picture before sending my address. Back in the living room, I checked on the footage - 58% uploaded - and grabbed the tin, rolling a joint as quickly as I could. On the balcony, I burnt the end and took long, hard drags.

"You smoked without us?"

I looked back. Leo and Cara, stood pretty close to each other. His face was kind of dumbfounded. Maybe even a bit hurt.

"I didn't use much. I have someone coming over so thought I'd jump ahead."

Leo stepped out. Cara took the silent cue to stay behind.

"Who's coming over?"

I shrugged nonchalantly.

"We've never met."

I swiped my phone from my pocket. Leo turned silent and withdrawn and stalked back inside to roll with Cara. I felt his apprehension. Hell, I felt the same thing in my own bones. But I couldn't just rely on one person to take care of all my needs, it was obvious. I'd been stupid to think I could. We both needed other friends and probably some space, and God knows it had been a long time since I'd been touched by a man.

On my way back in, I checked the footage upload - 68% - and silently cursed that it wasn't a percentage point higher so I could have made a stupid joke and perhaps melt away some of the tension in the room. It felt like war and stalemate rolled into one. I didn't like it.

A deep rumble outside my window was interrupted by a shuffling of feet, and then the bright chimes of the electric doorbell. A pit opened wide in my stomach, then I slid open my bedroom door and raced to the front of the flat. In the mirror, I could see the reflection of Leo and Cara smoking outside. Neither of them looked happy or even content. It was depressing. Probably my fault.

On the other side of the creaky wooden door, 'John' (forum names only - we didn't divulge anything deeper than that) stood in an impatient yet expectant stance. I don't know how to describe such a position, but it's the energy he exuded.

"Hey."

"Hey."

I was out of practice.

I invited John into my room, quickly bypassing the frosty living room and Leo's stare, and shut us both into the silence. His face was nice. Good beard. Pretty eyes. Olive complexion. His aftershave was sprayed on heavy, and his hair was slicked back with gel which felt out of fashion but nostalgic, perhaps.

"I—"

Before another word came out of his mouth, I grabbed the nape of his neck and pulled him into a kiss. I didn't want to hear about his life or his journey or his wants or needs. He was there as a purely physical presence, a means to an end, and I wanted him to settle into the role. It's not like I could direct the performance on my own. He needed to play his part, and from the limited context the forums offered, his words promised a straightforward, no-strings-attached encounter. If he went off-script, I'd invite him to leave.

I heard Leo and Cara laugh at a TV show in the living

room. I knew the episode and the series off-by-heart. It was one that Leo and I rewatched all the time when we got a bit too high. There was something comforting about knowing how it all played out.

When John started sucking on the tip of my dick, I realised I was completely zoning out of this encounter. I had to play my part too, so I grabbed his head and forced it down and spat out some words of encouragement which made his throat open up.

The canned laughter from the TV intertwined with the real life giggles outside the door, and it made me angrier and more intent on putting on a show. I wanted them both to know how uncomfortable I felt, isolated, heartbroken. But this man would make it better. It would seem like I was okay.

My emotions were a mess. Things were easier when you just focused on physical sensations.

John and I bent, rubbed, entered, sucked, twisted, groaned and shook our way to climax. I said thank you and kept my conversation short so he'd get the message to leave. As it always does, the post-coital chat drew on too long, so I answered every expected question with to-the-point words.

"I did, did you? No I don't know them. That would be fun. I'm not dating but maybe we could do this again. I don't have cash for a taxi. You can have the Wifi code to hail a cab if you want. I'd like that. Sure. Yep. Bye."

I released John from my room and directed him to let himself out. I didn't put a t-shirt on because I wanted Leo to see my sweat glisten in the dim tungsten light. As soon as he noticed me, I shrunk back behind my door.

The laughing stopped, and I heard the front door close again an hour later. Footsteps tracked out in the hall and stopped by my door for just a moment, before continuing into Leo's room.

Good wasn't really a good descriptor for how I felt. Comfortably empty was a better one, both in emotion and physical capacity. There was a spark missing which I hoped would come back after rest, but just in case it didn't, I decided to scan the forums and see if anything weird or fucked up was happening.

It wasn't until 3:00am that I remembered Kat's funeral was first thing in the morning.

Fuck.

I tossed and turned all night. My only thought was whether they found any more of her skin to put in the coffin.

CHAPTER 10

The coffee I made went cold, and Leo didn't touch his cup at all. My tie felt strange around my neck, and for a moment or two I considered stringing myself over the balcony, fashioning the fabric into a personal stripy noose. I'd either suffocate or fall and splatter, but both options would burn my memory into people's minds. I guess I had death on the brain.

Leo eventually surfaced, the space under his eyes black and baggy. His gaze was intermittent, friendly but noncommittal. I told him he didn't have to come, he didn't even know Kat. I didn't even really know her. But he said he wanted to come, wanted to be there for me, which raised a hundred questions I didn't have time to ponder the answers to.

In the car, we listened to music with the windows down and shared fragments of conversations, but it was all just rehashed filler. The grid-like grey of the city streets eventually transitioned into winding country lanes, a little taste of nature to break up the heavy melancholy.

Leo was trapped in his mind today, but he'd get over it.

The lines of our friendship had been drawn, and I wouldn't press the issue. Nor would I hide my natural tendency to self-destruct and sleep with any guy who gave me a quick passing glance. It was the way we were built, deep down, and we could never escape that. I don't know why I ever tried to pretend otherwise.

"I didn't realise you felt—" Leo muttered out of nowhere, and then stopped himself. He didn't speak another word on the journey, but did bob his head to one of our favourite rock tracks.

The usual suspects showed up to the funeral. Bob and Shelly and Todd, of course, but also extended family and their respective mistresses, widowers, and friends of friends. The service was fine: a nice, expected level of monotony with hymns and tears and regrets. Only two people made conversation about the weird circumstances of Kat's death after the service: a girl called Lynn (an unfortunate name for someone so young), and Toni, twin girls who were both friends of the dearly departed.

"It's just so weird. It doesn't make sense."

"Kat wouldn't just wander off. She was kidnapped for sure."

"I agree. And what happened—surely it wasn't human. Her flesh was… mangled, apparently."

"We think it's supernatural, right Lynn?"

The two girls had their own back and forth going on, I didn't need to interrupt. I just listened as new tidbits of information seeped from their chatter. It wasn't important but it felt respectful to hear them out. Leo was talking to my dad over by his car, and I guess I should have probably made more effort to introduce them before such an awkward first meeting. They seemed to be getting on, though, so I figured I could listen to the depresso sisters a little longer.

A text buzzed onto my phone. Mani—best friend in name but someone I kept in decreasingly regular contact with.

"Me and Kasey send our condolences. Want to grab a beer and hang later?"

I'd usually make up an excuse and tell them I was busy or sick or a mixture of both. But today I needed some space. I wrote a rushed reply and headed over to Dad.

"Hey Dad. I've made plans to see Kasey and Mani so am gonna have to head off. They send their condolences."

Dad nodded. Leo shuffled to the side and let us talk.

"You all good? You look super tired," I noted, staring at his increasingly wrinkly and textured face.

"There's some stuff going on behind the scenes. I'm working on something that I can't talk about, but it's driving me crazy. Listen, be careful with your filming, something's not right down at the pier."

"You saw the video?"

He nodded.

The small talk wrapped up and Leo and I were back in the car, heading back to the overcast coast.

"I didn't realise you were going out," Leo stuttered.

"Me neither. Kind of last minute."

"Can we talk?"

The sentence hung unanswered in the air for a moment.

"Let's talk later."

— — — —

Me, Mani, and Kasey. The saddest version of the three musketeers you could imagine. We met on the rooftop of our favourite building in town, a dilapidated two-storey shop that'd had a broken fire door for over three years. Easy access. It was built in the same brutalist style as the central library, and was quite honestly a rotting, diseased structure begging to be knocked down and rebuilt. Maybe next time, the architects would consider some colour or a different material to give it at least an air of friendliness. There was comfort in the mess though.

The three of us were folding sheets of plain A4 paper into aeroplanes whilst talking about our ambitions. I'd never been one to really plan or anything, but it felt right to daydream for a bit. And do something with my hands that wasn't smoking or jerking off.

I was the first to launch my plane. It soared a few metres, before a gust of air caught the left wing, sending it swirling in a haze of beige. It eventually crashed into the window of an office building, crumpling into a distorted bunch. It landed hard on the street below.

Kasey was next.

She let go of the plane, right after mentioning she'd whittled down her choice of job to veterinarian or doctor. I said that those paths were quite different, despite the obvious similarities, and she'd have to decide soon before like a decade of study. Kasey didn't think too hard about it. She was the kind of girl to dream but not take action. I had no doubts about her ability, but thought it more likely she'd end up as a receptionist at a GP surgery or vet, as opposed to the main role. Her plane didn't even make it a metre before crash landing.

Mani let go of his plane next. It soared further than mine, and was caught by another gust of air which propelled it up and over one of the student accommodation buildings opposite. We all clapped gently.

"Did you guys hear that weird sound the other day? It broke my window."

It was a weird question to ask, but for some reason the whole afternoon felt strange in their company. I needed to break the ice a bit and keep talking before I started to analyse why we were even friends.

"I heard it's terrorist cells," Mani said. "Gathering information to plot an attack."

"Hmm."

"Didn't you say on the group chat that someone was acting weird downstairs?" he asked.

My ears pricked up. I didn't remember saying that. My sent messages said otherwise. I was probably intoxicated.

"Yeah. I forgot I even wrote that. I've been a bit distant and weird."

Mani nodded slyly.

"Standard behaviour lately."

Ouch. I wanted to apologise and explain that things were strange because my cousin was dead (though we weren't close), and me and Leo weren't talking, and he'd found a girl which basically meant there was no chance at all that things could carry on as I wanted them to. But that was a lot of information to process at once, so instead I said nothing at all.

I grabbed another sheet of paper, structured it in the traditional way, but then added a couple of stray folds. I didn't have a plan for what would happen, nor did I expect anything in particular from the extra flourish. But as I launched it over the threshold, it danced in the air, did a loop and came to a soft landing on the balcony of the student flats in front of us. The gentle claps returned. A small sense of pride. I'd have taken even the smallest amount of recognition in that moment. It felt good.

As I tracked back to the balcony, searching for the final resting place of my paper vehicle, I saw a silhouette of a guy. He was around our age. Long, dark hair. That's all I could make out. Aside from the fact he was naked, dick swinging and all, in a display that could easily count as indecent exposure.

He was staring right at us, trying to get our attention.

"We don't need it!" he screamed, his voice hoarse and pained. Immediately following the outburst, he pointed up at the sky with a kitchen knife.

"It's better in their possession!"

I shook my head. I hacked up some phlegm and spat it down to the street.

"We don't know what you mean."

"Just like Bobby said! On his post! It's all for them and for us too. We don't need it!"

"Who the fuck's Bobby?" Mani shouted, to no response.

I can't say the guy smiled, because he was too far away. But he perked up. Raising his left arm up high, knife in his right hand, he started shearing the flesh away from his bone. Kasey and Mani recoiled in disgust as a fountain of blood erupted from his wrists, raining down crimson onto the unsuspecting people at street level. I was just in awe.

The stranger didn't panic. Didn't scream. Didn't have much of a reaction at all. Instead, he peeled away a strip of flesh like a slice of lamb doner and threw it over his balcony.

"It doesn't hurt! Doesn't even feel pain!"

He cackled. Spat. Screamed. After trying to shear away another segment of his arm, he lost his footing, feet slipping on the growing pool of blood beneath him. After an almost comical attempt at regaining balance, his body folded over the safety rail, and free-falled through the weightless air.

The boy's body slopped to the ground, repainting the dull architecture of the surrounding buildings with a red spray. Kasey and Mani were losing their shit. I was trying to decide how to word this on the forums. It was an important development, and I kicked myself for not having my camera with me.

"What do we do?" Mani panicked.

I saw a chrome van speed towards the body, a giant orange coil packed on the back, the same kind as the one on the beach before. One of the plastic-suited people jumped out and started hosing down the body. He picked through the blood, as if looking for something. Then—the sound of sirens.

The enigmatic character packed up and sped off, eyes tracking the environment for any issues. An ambulance arrived just after. It all seemed strangely choreographed. I made one more plane whilst watching, and it landed in some stagnant blood right by one of the paramedics. He looked up at us in disgust.

— — — —

F/ Portsmouth [latest]
u/ exuberantecstasyespresso: Rising death toll
It's all happening. Anyone who has been over to the F/weirduk thread knows about the cryptic messages that have been posted over the last couple of weeks. Are we going to

pretend that nothing is happening still?

The latest death was a young guy today in town. Jumped or fell from student accommodation. I heard from a paramedic friend that his head was full of some kind of weird yellow substance. Drugs? A weird new dangerous trend? Who the fuck knows. But the police need to start taking it seriously.

-

—> u/ *mamaMartina:*
It's the fungus, isn't it? We have a problem on our hands.

-

u/ *exuberantecstasyespresso:*
What fungus?

-

— —> u/ Josh4265ab:
We saw this boy. He mentioned something about a post from someone called Bobby. Do you know who that is?

-

u/ *exuberantecstasyespresso:*
Yeah. Check the link - f/weirduk.co/1299839

— — — —

F/ weirduk [top]
u/bobbybobbybobby: Clarity

I was the first one in the water. The first one to get the "disease". It's not disease. It's enlightenment. You're missing the point. All of you. Idiots.

They're coming for us. I'm sure of it. After I was in the water. They need it. They want it. The vehicles up ahead. Want to take us away. I tell everyone same thing. Get in water. Get in there. We don't need our skin. They do. They want to take us up, make us live good lives. We'll get new skin. Sacrifice what we have now for better lives. That's all everyone wants right?

Go to the beach now. Don't stay away. Go there and don't look back. We need to sacrifice to show we're ready. Are you ready? I am. I show them every day with a slice of skin and pouring blood and a smile on my face, and everyone who is dead might already be there.

-

—> u/ *sheebal123:*

You need a fucking doctor.

-

— —> u/ ahnayyon123:

Didn't we already report this guy for this shit?

-

—> u/ *sheebal123:*

I suppose it is called 'weirduk'.

-

u/ *bobbybobbybobby:*

I don't need a doctor. I just need to spread this message. Help me spread it.

-

— —> u/ ahnayyon123:

Fucking nutcase. @mods can we block this idiot?

-

u/ *bobbybobbybobby:*

Fuck you cunts. If anyone reads. Go to beach. Do it. Go and get clarity. Then come to the house. Come with us. New life. New skin. Come.

[user u/ bobbybobbybobby has been blocked] - mod team

CHAPTER 11

The city was a fucking mess.

The next morning, I passed Leo a coffee. He leant forward from the sofa and took it with both hands, resting the laptop on the table in front of him.

"I'm sorry," I said, not a hundred percent sure why, but it felt like the right thing to do.

"You don't need to be sorry. I just wasn't sure what was going on."

"Because I slept with a guy? I told you about all my hookups when we talked." I reminded him.

He nodded.

"It was just unexpected. We were having a good time talking and filming, and suddenly—"

I'd been shaking my head as a natural reaction. I didn't realise it was quite so obvious.

"Listen, Leo. I'm glad you found Cara and you're doing well at the job and that. But I just feel—"

"Cara and me aren't anything. Why would you think that?"

My heart dropped.

"What do you mean? You invited her over randomly, and said she was hot when she interviewed you."

Leo took a sip of his coffee.

"I don't know what I feel honestly. But it's nothing like what you're thinking. We aren't even talking after the other night. I don't think she enjoyed herself."

"I'm sorry." I meant it.

"I'm not. She was nice enough, but pretty fucking dull. We didn't… you know. Go all the way."

Now I felt like an idiot who jumped to conclusions.

And Leo was sorry. He seemed to mean it too.

"I just don't ever want to feel like I can't talk to you," he continued. "That fucking sucked. I would never let anyone come between our friendship, and I'd like to think you feel the same."

I nodded slowly.

"Of course I do"

"Right then. Stop being such a twat and let's get editing."

I giggled. That was that. We tracked through every second of footage from the other night, and pieced together a rough cut of the weird boy on the beach. We got some great establishing shots of the pebbles and water, dynamic footage of Leo talking to camera, and then the pièce de résistance… The boy poking his dirty fingers into various abscessed crevices.

"It's fucking vile," I decided. "When do we upload it?"

Leo gave the whole thing a bit of a spruce up—he was getting good at this whole editing thing—and it was ready. So we uploaded it to the forums and across our socials, ready for a new wave of mysteries and comments. Our following had been growing at an unexpected rate, and it seemed like every time we logged on, there were legions of new followers getting up to speed and asking their own questions. The attention felt good.

Whilst we waited for reactions, the two of us got in the kitchen and started cooking. We'd shared so many meals, so many packets of ramen and microwave fare, but we never really *cooked* all that much. But the wind took us in a different direction, so we grabbed what we had and put it together in a haphazard yet inspired way.

Hours later, we cleaned our plates whilst sat on the sofa, feeling full and kinda satisfied. Our mouths were drawn to the food, our eyes to the laptop screen. The comments were coming in thick and fast.

— — — —

F/ Portsmouth [latest]
u/ LE02019xyk: Portsmouth Mystery. Part 2
Me and [Josh4265ab] shot a second video in our new series of mini docs. This was an encounter with a guy around our age down the pier. Content warning: Blood and disease.

LINK: www.gofetchvid.com/beachboy1

-

—> u/ rorythetory221
What the fuck? Is he on something?

-

——> u/ jon_underscore_name
I love this video series, even though it only has two parts. I'm not in Portsmouth but these guys are good. Please do more!

-

————> u/ *cara_mathers_2*

You didn't credit me for sound. Douchebags.

-

—————> u/ *adbject*

Who's investigating this? These boys are doing more work than the actual police.

-

——————> u/ *mamaMartina:*

Who else has heard about the fungus? We need to start investigating and talking about this. Please DM me as I'm unable to DM you from a newly made account.

— — — —

"Looks like we need a part three," Leo said.

I agreed. I didn't know how far this mystery went, but it felt right to be covering it.

"What if we went out tonight?"

"Tonight?"

Leo had that look in his eye again. The one that told me he was keen to go and do something right away. The sparkle that told me I wouldn't be arguing with him about this, and even if I tried, I'd lose.

I decided to take him up on the offer, and went to go shower first. The hot water felt good on my body, wiping away the grime and the anxiety of the last few days. Kasey and Mani had sent me a few text messages, but they all went pretty much unread. They were taking the guy's death weirdly, talking about PTSD and shit. I just thought of it as another day and another weird event. It didn't have any lasting effect on me, not really. When one of your own parents has taken their life right in front of your eyes —blaming every single issue leading up to the moment on you too—everything else feels kind of blunt and distant.

The heat from the shower still resided in my skin as I wrapped the towel around my waist and opened the door, unleashing a plume of steam into the living area. Before I had a chance to get to my room, I noticed Leo standing by the front door.

"What's up?"

"I'm just thinking."

"Thinking about what?" I asked.

He turned to me, a look of deep confusion burned into his eyes.

"Thinking about why I didn't do this before."

I didn't have a chance to question things - his hands were already around the back of my head, pulling me in for a kiss. His touch was desperate, feral. He held me in place, kissing me and taking over my entire being. I thought of every conversation we'd had, every moment we'd spent together, and how I didn't expect any of it to lead to this. Not in my wildest dreams.

He let go, and I expected the 'mistake' talk. It quite often went like this:

"I'm sorry, I'm confused and my emotions got caught up, but I'm definitely straight. You can't tell any of my friends about this. Or my girlfriend. Oh my god. I didn't think—what we did was wrong and you're not to ever repeat it okay? I swear to God if you do—" Blah blah blah.

But he didn't. Instead, he stripped his shirt off, grabbed me by the shoulders and pushed me onto the sofa. Lying with him there, skin on skin, felt right and overdue. We kissed more, then tugged our dicks until we shared stickiness and a secret that would be committed to memory. It was the first time we'd really let each other in. It was a moment I wouldn't forget.

In that embrace, in that intimate state, things were perfect, even if only for a moment.

CHAPTER 12

Things were back to normal. We were both full of adrenaline and questions and answers, not pertaining to the night's events but to the world at large. Like the first time we met, we were curious about every single thread of life.

I'd packed my camera and a spare battery, plus the mic and light. Leo tied his hair back and put on a nice shirt. We were getting into pro-mode for our videos. We weren't sure what we were looking for exactly, but the best content came from discovery, rather than pre-planning. I might have made that up, but it's what I was sticking with.

Using the LED light, we hovered around the beach and the pier, intermittently climbing closer to the water to see if anyone was around. It was a quiet night. Wind swept the waves with a gentle whistle. Cackling groups of kids drank cheap cider. A dog barked somewhere by the park. I wasn't sure exactly what we'd expected, but nothing was happening.

But then, we noticed some kind of substance floating atop the frothy waves. It was impossible to ascertain what it was under a blanket of darkness, but it definitely wasn't meant to be floating in public water.

Leo perched up at the side of the shore, ensuring that both he and the water were in frame. It wasn't much to go on, but we decided to give it a go.

"Be careful. You're right by the edge," I warned.

"One kiss and you think you can look after me, dude?" he joked.

I tutted then started rolling.

"Okay. Good to go. Make up some fun shit."

Leo started reeling off information about the beach, the weird enigmatic substance, and basically painted a picture that made the whole situation seem more exciting than it really was. That was a good talent. He could spin anything to make it instantly alluring. Good or bad.

Sickly amber light from the pier refracted against his face, lighting him up in abstract patterns. Teetering on the edge of the pebbled beach, water caressing the edge, it felt cinematic.

"I want to go up there," Leo said.

"No. It's too high."

"It will look good though. The angle and shit."

"Leo—"

I lost again.

The newly-built sea defence structures consisted of jagged rock formations running around the perimeter of the beach, angled razors of distressed grey built in messy yet calculated piles. Not safe for climbing or presenting amateur video shows from, that's for sure. But under the soft glint of moonlight and a dulling LED, Leo pulled his frame atop the surface, waved, and told me to start rolling.

"Mate! Be careful."

Leo nodded. Shrugged it off. I set down the tripod, and

extended the mic as far as it would go. Maybe having an extra sound person wasn't such a bad idea for future shoots. Not Cara though. Fuck her.

"This city is alight with rumours. You've seen the fish. The boy. The guy that jumped from the student accommodation. We can't ignore this anymore."

A deep gurgle arose from the sea. Bobbing silhouettes let out human growls, followed by laughter. I turned the camera on Leo's order, and noticed several floating heads, facial features hidden in shadow. Their bodies were submerged. Leo started shouting questions at them, whilst I silently questioned how they weren't all dead from hypothermia. I was three-layers deep and still ice at my core.

As the strangers started to bob towards the shore, I noticed the complete lack of any particular shared demographic. They were people of all ages, genders, races, a friendship group unlike any other. This was either a weird prank, a night-time swimming club, or something much more minacious. Against every instruction in the self-help book I was listening to, I went for the scarier, more fear-based option.

An older woman settled closest to us, her face illuminated by my shaky light. Her eyes were milky, glazed over. Her face looked covered in some kind of orange moss with streaks of blood and discharge.

"I'll wear this a bit longer," she groaned, her rotten teeth on display as her flaky lips caught on her gums. The sentence was completely incomprehensible. Not only was the woman completely naked (judging by the sagging bags of flesh floating in front of her body) but her mouth moved in disjointed, haunting ways.

"Get a closer frame!" Leo called out.

I was fully zoomed in, the woman's face filling the tiny LCD screen on my camera. I took a couple of steps forward, tracking the scene and the various faces and afflictions.

In the middle of the water, the boy from the other night was making steady progress in the apathetic race to the shore. His abscessed skin now completely covered his face and neck, juicy crevices seeping into the water.

"It's time!" the boy gargled, staring at me with dark, pit-like eyes.

"Josh!" Leo called.

Suddenly, Leo lost his footing and careened down onto the rocks with a thump. His shoes slipped as he tried to stand, and blood oozed from his shoulder. He'd sliced up the fancy shirt he'd picked out an hour before.

Moments later, he was in the water, a spray of murky green jetting around him on impact. I heard him gulp and gasp, as the strangers floated closer to his jerking body.

"LEO!"

He could neither see nor hear me. He was panicking.

I discarded the camera, took off my shoes, got ready to dive in after him. But a bright light cut through the darkness, burnt away the plans I had in mind. Emergency sirens erupted behind me, just as I saw the old woman try and push Leo's head underwater. His hair was slicked around his face, eyes bulging, hands wrung into fists as they punched at the water.

"Don't go in there!"

A familiar voice.

My eyes adjusted to the night. I saw my Dad in his uniform, running from the car.

"DAD!"

"Josh?"

"Help him!"

The strangers in the water started to howl, cackling between breaths. The rotting woman screamed in pleasure as her bingo-wing arms wrapped around Leo, trying to drown him. He was underwater now. I wasn't thinking straight. I grabbed a handful of rocks and threw them as hard as I could at her face. Most of them splatted against the water, one hit Leo in the shoulder (*shit*), but one or two connected, squashing her saggy skin with blunt trauma. I couldn't see much, but it was enough to stop her making noise and push her away for a moment.

"Get back!"

Dad sprinted over, intercepting me, and grabbed a life ring. In a practiced motion, he threw it towards Leo. After a bit more thrashing, Leo grabbed on tight, and we both helped pull him back. The strangers didn't try to grab Leo or the ring, instead settling back into the background, returning to the abyss and all of its enigmatic secrets.

— — — —

We sat in the back of the police car, drying off whilst waiting for the paramedics. I grabbed the camera and the equipment on the way to the vehicle, but wasn't sure how much we'd captured. My adrenaline was still pumping. I could feel it in my skin, a gentle but kind of exciting pressure. Leo looked the same. Panic over. Happy to be alive.

"Who the fuck were they?"

Leo shook his head.

"New subjects for the video, I guess."

The paramedics didn't show up for an hour, but after a

quick check-up, we opted for a ride with my Dad. We invited him in but duty called, and as I reached in to give him a hug, I noticed a patch of yellow on the outer crease of his eyelid. He explained it was nothing to worry about, hugged me tighter, and wished us a good night.

"I'm looking into something, but it's a big case with lots of moving parts. Just stay away from the water, okay?"

They were his last words before he drove away and we retreated back into our house.

The city felt cold. Unsafe. Breached, in some way. We rushed in and took turns in the shower, acclimating to the flat and the only place that felt safe that night.

— — — —

F/ Portsmouth [latest]
u/portsmouthjacob: Anyone seen this?

The weird post on the forum earlier had a link to this. Anyone know what it is?

PLANS FOR ███████

███████████████████████████████████████

████████████████████ ███████████

████████████████ ████████████████████

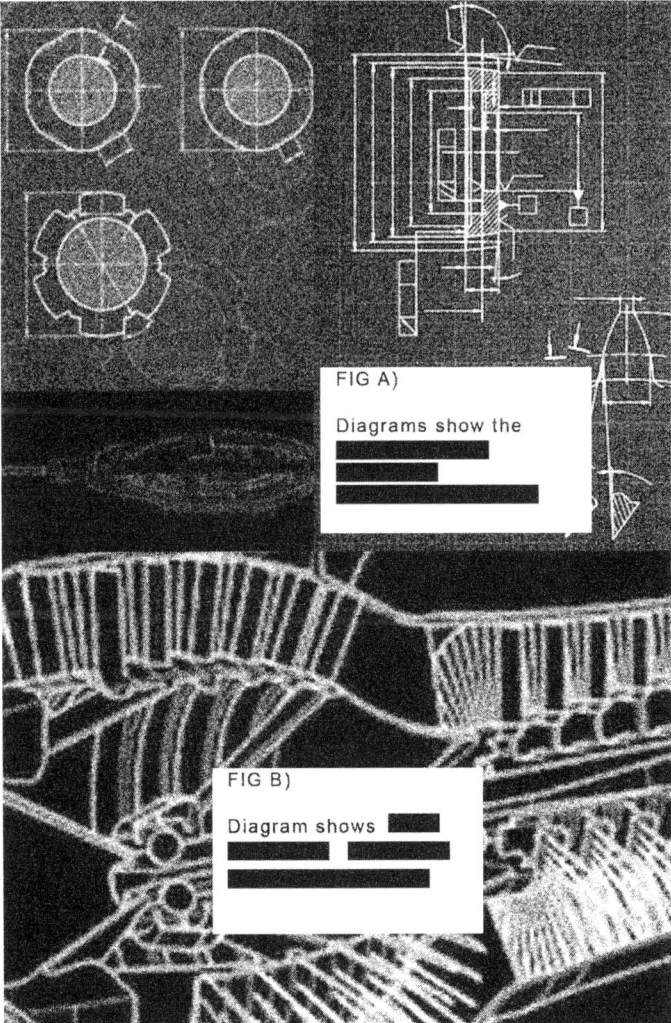

FIG A)

Diagrams show the
████████████
██████████████████████

FIG B)

Diagram shows ████████
████████████ ████████████
████████████████████████

CHAPTER 13

I woke up to a hacking cough. 2:59am. The sound transitioned into my reality softly, in the way that waking from a dream often does. The cough wasn't mine but Leo's. We were sharing a bed; warming up was our excuse. There were no repeats of our intimate moment; the events of the night were all we could think about.

In the kitchen, I poured Leo a glass of water and stared outside the window for a bit, wondering whether those people might still be down the beach, or if they also had homes to go and sleep in at night. Back in my room, Leo was twisted onto his side, his breath rapid and restless. I slid my hand onto his shoulder, it was cold and sticky. The gash from the rocks was covered in a bandage, but seemed to be healing up okay.

"I feel like dog shit," he whispered.

"You look like it too," I teased.

I laid awake with him, grabbing the glass of water when he needed it, offering words of comfort in between calling him a crybaby and a loser to make him laugh. A notification rang up on my phone.

"What's that?" he asked, not turning to look.

"I got a headshot booking. I completely forgot I even had the page live still. It's been ages since I marketed myself."

I checked out the details. An older woman. Scientist. Wanted a nice headshot for her website and an upcoming book. It had been a while, but I had all the equipment I needed to make it happen.

"Oh shit... It's tomorrow."

"That's quite sudden," Leo pitched in.

I nodded, following it up verbally because he couldn't see me.

"She's offering five hundred quid up front though, so I'll do whatever she needs me to."

A pause...

"Saying shit like that is how people end up tied up in a basement and used as sex toys," he joked. I slapped his arm, apologised for grazing his cut, and fell asleep with a smile on my face.

— — — —

The city was quiet. Too quiet.

The bed was drenched when I woke up. Leo had tossed and turned and coughed up God knows what through the night. I basically peeled myself out of the sheets.

Breakfast was buttered toast whilst charging my batteries. I slurped tea and sucked crumbs from wet fingers, then packed my bags. On the way out of the flat, I called the arcade and told them Leo wouldn't be in. They sighed and said that most of the staff were off and asked if he'd be okay to do a half-day. I didn't have time to negotiate my friend's work schedule, so I hung up and blamed it on the signal.

The world outside the building felt like melancholy personified. A humdrum scattering of people walked around like NPCs, directionless but in motion. The worst kind of combination. The usually welcome smell of damp rain in the air felt oppressive and suffocating, and every sound seemed to compete with every other.

When had everything got so fucking grey?

I loaded my bags into the car boot and started the engine. As I turned to look out the rear windscreen, I noticed a scratchy message drawn in blood and fish guts. I didn't have time to read it, instead just washed it away with a soapy jet of water and a few revolutions of the wipers. I immediately regretted not taking a quick peek.

— — — —

"Martina Jeffries. But you can call me Ma."

Kind of a weird introduction. I was still going to call her Martina.

It was a relief that the woman hadn't fallen into the trap that so many of my previous clients had in the past, by turning up in some stereotypical outfit that screamed amateur or rudimentary. Had she turned up in a white lab coat with some beakers and bunsen burners as props, I'd have politely told her to fuck off.

Instead, she had a range of simple outfits, and didn't mind getting changed in her car. Her personality seemed nice enough: professional, straightforward. But there was something under the layers, something itching to get out.

I asked her some questions about her life, her work, and she gave me the polite version: short, to the point and ready to wrap up at any sign of boredom.

"You can angle your body slightly. It will make it look less flat."

She followed the direction.

"Lift your chin just a bit. And push forward through your forehead."

She did so. I took a few shots and reviewed them on-screen.

"This is going to sound weird," she mentioned. "But I've seen your videos."

I looked up from the camera.

"Videos?"

"From the beach."

"You have?"

"Yes. And I have another motive for being here today."

I nodded, sighing.

"You're still paying though, right?"

"Definitely. The pictures look great. And I really do need new headshots."

"Okay. So why are you here?"

Martina grabbed a flask of coffee. She offered me some but I declined. Taking small, gentle sips, she tried to decide how to broach the subject.

"The most recent video I saw was on a forum website. It was the one of the boy."

"Okay," I said, half-listening and half checking out the pictures I'd taken.

"Well, that's my son. And he hasn't been home in a week."

I let the camera dangle around my neck. Her face was sorrowful and complex.

"Your son? Did you tell the police?"

She nodded again, placed her flask down, and settled into her next pose. I lifted the camera, took the shot, reviewed. They all looked decent, but my mind was on the conversation.

"He's always enjoyed swimming. Usually first thing in the morning to get ready for the day. But something's wrong. I saw loads of strange posts on his computer. And then I saw the video, and—"

"I saw him again last night," I interrupted. "His friends tried to drown my housemate,"

I hit the trigger just as she leant towards me, eager for more information.

"Chin up," I said reflexively. Then, "Sorry. Let's take a break."

I took her up on the coffee, after all. We found a damp bench and sat on our coats. A half cup of milky caffeine each, and we were warming up to each other, talking casually. She told me about her boy, and I made sure not to tell her any of the disgusting things I'd seen him do (sticky abscess fingers still burned into my mind), though if she'd seen the video she knew already.

We reviewed the photos, agreed on five to edit into a final selection, and she transferred me the money on the spot. Martina was a new user on the forums, and asked if we could keep in touch via email instead. I said of course, and that she should send me any information she'd seen that could help our investigation. I don't know why I said that—I'm not a policeman, just a Z-list graduate photographer—but maybe we were helping bring more light to the subject in any case.

"It's much bigger than us. And it's going to keep spreading."

Those were her parting words. I nodded, waved her off, and packed my gear into the boot.

"And stay out of the water!" she added, head hung out of the driver's window as she accelerated away.

She didn't need to tell me that twice.

CHAPTER 14

The house was empty. There was evidence Leo had got up and left (the bed was kind of made and the bathroom steamed up from a shower), but I was confused where he might be. Definitely not the arcade (I'd already called them up) and nowhere around the hallways or common rooms in the flat.

I started editing the photos, adding in some contrast, taking away a little bit of skin texture. It was a fast process deftly executed, and I delivered the final files before the evening.

In return, Martina sent over a few links with some information and a few threads I'd missed between visits.

One stood out in particular.

— — — —

F/ Portsmouth [latest]

u/chanceitordont: My girlfriend is acting weird. Please help.

I've been keeping up with the news. And these threads. My girlfriend has some kind of weird rash on her face and neck. Her mind is elsewhere. The doctors won't listen and just keep giving us antibiotics. I need to know other people are struggling with this. I'm going to suggest a drug test but I don't know if that will work. She's angry. Hopeless. Manic. I'm losing the person I love.

EDIT: I suggested drug test. It didn't go well. I need to leave, I can't deal with it all right now.

EDIT 2: I just got a call that she's missing. I hope she's okay. She hasn't been back to her job at the arcade in days. Weeks maybe.

EDIT 3: If anyone knows a girl called Cara Mathers, tell her I need her home.

— — — —

That name. Cara Mathers. Leo's boss. The girl who came over and flirted and did whatever else with him. What the fuck?

Was she in an open relationship? Being weird and secretive? Whatever it was, she was missing, and it made me concerned for Leo. He already stressed there was nothing going on, but something felt off. This wasn't coming from a place of jealousy or lust, but actual fear.

There was a strange clattering sound in the distance.

"We don't need it. Not really. Not now."

The strange voice startled me. I didn't know that voice at all... and it came from just metres behind me.

I turned slowly, the air thickening as I pushed my body counterclockwise, breathing hard. My front door was resting in an open position, streaks of clotted blood spread from the handle to the peephole. Muddy tracks extended from the door to this stranger's feet, carried through by tatty trainers.

Moments later, I got a proper look at the stranger's face. Mid twenties. Rat-like face and big teeth. Definite overbite. His eyes were off-colour. Sour yellow.

"Who are you?"

The question sounded almost foreign in my head, like I was speaking words from somewhere else. An out of body experience.

"You write a lot on the forums. Make videos. Film us. You can film me."

I arched my head. Tried to recognise this stranger. But I couldn't place him.

"What do you want?" I asked.

He snarled and shook his head three times, more OCD than reacting to an itch or something.

"I want you to film me. I'm waiting for them. He said it was okay."

Anger built in my chest. A red-hot steam ready to fight. Or maybe give into flight. Who the fuck knew.

"You need to leave my house."

"But he invited me…."

I shook my head. Before I had a chance to move, the guy ran towards me, arms flailing. Reacting as quick as possible, I sidestepped, knocking my laptop from the kitchen counter to the ground. Adrenaline took over as I subconsciously reached for a knife from the spilled block.

"You need to leave."

"You read Bobby's post, right? You're always on the

forums. I see your videos and comments. We all believe it. That they're coming for us. You need to calm down. Come to the beach. We're gonna be rescued. Shame to leave you down here. We don't want that."

"Get the fuck back!" I screamed, waving the knife.

SQUELCH.

The stranger jumped forward, hands in the air. The blade sliced right into his stomach, a neat gash carved by metal. With a maniacal laugh, he withdrew, pulling his flesh from the knife, and pounced forward again, creating a brand new hole.

Unmoving, tears started to form in my eyes. But not in his. His eyes were steady. Focused… *Happy.*

It was impossible. He should have been writhing in pain. Blood and the contents of his stomach were already splashing out onto the kitchen tiles. Instead, his face was close to mine, disgustingly intimate, the warm body fluids pooling around the handle and my wrist. Carelessly, I let him step back, taking the weapon with him. It was still sticking out of him by the time Leo rushed through the entrance of the apartment.

"What the fuck?" Leo's voice. He was close, but I wasn't. I was miles away in my head, trying to detach from this very real, very disturbing nightmare.

"We're waiting for you!" the stranger spat. Without warning, he grabbed the knife handle, and started carving shapes in his abdomen, digging through gristle and bone in sickly motion.

"Stop that!" Leo screamed. He edged forwards, staring at the man and the floor in turn. The stranger ripped the knife out, let it tumble to the floor, and packed the cavity with a tea towel from the side.

I made eye contact with Leo. A somber apology waited

for me in his stare, but I was still in defence mode. Without tearing my eyes from him, I slid around the boundary of the kitchen, into the living room and finally my bedroom. I locked the door, shoved my desk chair in front of it, and completely broke down. It wasn't until I got into bed that I realised I was still covered in dirty crimson.

Sleep didn't come for hours. I heard arguments, screaming, the front door slamming shut. And then cupboards clattering, liquids pouring, the mop slapping against tile, muffled crying, and finally, Leo's door closing gently. When the coast was clear, I stepped into the dimly lit space, grabbed my phone and laptop—which now had a cracked screen, thanks stranger—and retreated to my room, desperately hoping that Leo wouldn't come out to talk.

It was the first night I felt unsafe in my own house. As if to cement the fact, blood-curdling screams rippled from outside my window not once but twice that night.

— — — —

F/ Portsmouth [latest]
u/ lastchanceraj: IT HAPPENED

You guys probably know Bobby over on f/ weirduk. He got banned from here. And then there. It doesn't matter. It happened tonight. Like he planned. He didn't have much flesh left. Kept cutting, slicing, dicing. Blood all over the house. I want to follow him. He found them, went out there on his own. They were over the garden. Bright lights and ZAP he was gone, just a bit of skin left. He's up there now. Probably looking down on us. We need to follow his word. Keep going. Keep on going. This isn't about just one of us. It's about us all. The next level of human race. Come to beach. Stop fucking around. Join us. You can feel it after the water.

CHAPTER 15

"That's insane. Impossible actually. Did you call the hospital? The police?"

I studied Martina's wrinkled face from across the table, taking in the strangely cosy vibes of the café. It was situated on Palmerston Road, a vaguely busy thoroughfare which sometimes housed a market but today was empty and cold. Thankfully, the café was relatively warm and friendly. It's why I picked it as a spot to meet.

"Leo said he'd take care of it. I—"

I didn't finish the sentence. I couldn't bear to think about what was going on. Truthfully, I'd tried to call my Dad around 3:00am, but I think he was on duty, so I left a message or three instead. As I drifted into memories and remembered the stranger carving his own abdomen, it wasn't long until I was back to the campsite, remembering the elderly man and his flappy bacon-skin peeled from his face…

I needed to focus. I counted to five. Tried that thing you're meant to do in a panic attack, where you name a decreasing amount of things that you can see, hear, and smell, but then gave up and just burned my tongue on shit coffee.

Martina looked at me somberly.

"Are you sure you want to do this?" I asked her. She nodded softly.

Ever since I'd mentioned seeing her son—was it Tommy? Thomas? I couldn't remember—at the beach, she'd been asking if I wanted to help her look for him. At the same time, she wanted to take some samples of the water to test, and I agreed it would probably be a good idea. I floated the idea of filming it, but the idea of doing a video without Leo was kind of sad so I left my equipment at home and said maybe another time.

Whilst I sipped my coffee, I tuned in to the clashing conversations happening around me. An older woman was talking about giving her dog his pills, and how she had to wrap them in ham to trick him to eat them. Classic. I'd fall for that if I was a dog.

Then there were two girls deciding on birthday gifts for a third, presumably absent, friend. One guy was closing a deal of some kind, feigning a life of luxury whilst he worked at a small corner table in this little establishment. But then two middle-aged women, probably about Martina's age, stole my focus.

"It's like he isn't even in that body any more. He's angry. Disgusting. Saying that he doesn't want to be on this planet anymore—"

I snapped back to reality. Stopped eavesdropping. I excused myself to order more coffee, gulped it down on the way back from the queue, and slipped on my coat ready to visit the beach.

Three missed calls and seven messages sat on my lock

screen. All from Leo. I'd previewed some of the text. My memory recalled fragments of several messages.

"It isn't what I thought—"

"Friendship means more to me than some kind of—"

"Disgusting and my head is a fucking mess but I need—"

"Please call and talk and I can explain because right now I'm fucking tired and I can't—"

I wasn't ready to properly engage with any of it. Hell, my other internet tabs were open on local hotels and places to stay, just in case I needed somewhere else to crash. Things had got really upside down and weird, and I needed to fucking scream or cry or sleep forever or something. But none of those were an option at the time, so instead I smiled at Martina and invited her to join me in my car, and we headed straight to the beach.

Isolated. Cold. The city operated in regular, predictable cycles. People were at work or school or dead perhaps, so there weren't many of them at the beach. We spent half an hour in the car, driving up and down, in search of Tommy (it was Tommy, not Thomas) but he wasn't around. I suggested that maybe he'd gone home back into the warm, regained his bearings. I didn't believe a word, but I had to try and be optimistic for once.

We pulled up to the car park outside the Rock Gardens, a strange miniature oasis of plants and wildlife at the edge of beach. It was both a fun area for families to spend time in the day and a gay cruising spot at night (I'd had a few encounters there myself). Neither demographic were there at the moment, which offered a chance for the birds and wild animals to relax and enjoy the scenery without being threatened by small children or the sight of saggy men fellating each other.

Martina grabbed clear jars and beakers and science things from her boot, and I offered to help carry some bits down to the shore. When we got there, she put on some gloves and carefully captured water from the edge of the sea, mindful not to contaminate herself or the other equipment. She mentioned something about not filling up the beakers all the way because she could spill some when opening it back at home, but her voice kind of dissolved in the void of my head. I hope she didn't find me rude. I was just preoccupied.

We drove for another fifteen minutes up and down Clarence Parade (the long road by the beach) looking for signs of her son, then called it a day. I dropped her back to her car, and stopped for a milkshake on the way to my flat. I couldn't decide whether to head back or just take the backpack I'd prepared to a hotel for the night. Let things settle down, as if all of this shit would just reverse in a night. But maybe after sleeping I'd be in a better position to tackle it. Fuck knows.

My next stop was the hill. Not for burgers, but for a quiet place to smoke a joint. I stopped in a car park, walked to the edge of the hill, and overlooked the city: twinkling lights, low hum of traffic, light sprinkling of rain. From up there, it looked almost picturesque. Beautiful. Of course, take a closer look and it was layers of shit on shit, a real dump aside from a few nuggets of gold, but that was just the UK and the world in general, I think. I don't know. I didn't really travel much.

I inhaled clouds under the clouds, letting the smoke

seep from my lungs in gentle exhales. The twinkling lights started to refract and dance a little, and I swore under my lungs because I was definitely too high to drive. There was a hotel a few minutes down the road, and I was all but set to check-in for the night. But a text appeared on my phone. A peace offering of sorts from Leo. He'd bought wine and takeaway curry and wondered if I wanted to watch some vintage horror films and chill out.

It didn't take too long to decide. With a dwindling bank account, a sore back and a heavy head, it made sense to stay in my own house. And I'd enjoy the evening without any questioning or dark vibes, and tackle the nonsense I called my life in the morning.

I got in my car, stalled a couple times, then took the long way home to ensure no-one would catch me driving high. It was reckless, selfish, and stupid. But in the grand scheme of things, I made it home safe without anything happening, so I said thank you to the universe and hopped into the apartment.

Leo embraced me with teary eyes and a strong grip. He smelled great. Our favourite aftershave. He'd showered and dressed in something nice, and his demeanour was apologetic and sincere. I relaxed on the sofa whilst he cooked and poured wine, we laughed the night away with moments hidden behind the cushions (some vintage horror was downright twisted), and when it came time for bed, he joined me in my room.

We fumbled drunkenly under the quilt until he begged me to let him take things up a notch, and before I knew it he was inside me and his body was the most mind-blowing experience I'd ever had. If you'd asked me in the post-coital glow if I loved that man and wanted to spend the rest of my life with him, I'd have said yes in a heartbeat. We slept in each other's arms, entangled and warm and far away from the beach or the deaths or the forums and everything in between. Under that quilt, we were safe and protected, and things were dreamlike until 3:00am. Then he started hacking and spewing and punching the wall in fits of rage.

I got him water and squeezed him tight, trying my best to take away the anger and rage and pessimism, but he kept on talking about how his flesh didn't fit and that maybe it was best if he went back to his room as he needed some space. I turned on the light and his eyes were bloodshot and kind of milky, and as he slunk back out into the hall, I tried to decide whether it was worth heading to a hotel after all. I fell asleep to a final text message from him, which buzzed through an hour or so later.

LEO

I'm sorry. Let's talk in the morning x

— — — —

F/ Portsmouth [latest]
u/ *xxddaa33453q: You're all wrong.*
You keep searching for your missing. You keep telling the news that we're mad or on drugs or at risk of harming ourselves. But you have no idea. Want the truth? It's at the beach. Don't listen to the radio. Newspapers. Any of that. Think of up there. What they're thinking. Something is coming. Only a few of us are ready. Don't say we didn't warn you.

-

—> u/ *janjonesloverka3*

is that jack? we're all worried. your mum's here now. give her a call.

-

__—─> u/ *xxddaa33453q*__

forget about me. i'm already done. happier. happiest. need to worry about yourselves. go to the beach. we might meet again if you do. tell her that. xo

CHAPTER 16

My head was ringing. The sun was bright. Too fucking bright through the gap in my blinds. I checked my phone. I was hoping Dad would have called or texted or something, but the man was AWOL. If ever I needed breakfast and a chat, it was today.

I had another headshot booking. It was for some uni grad and his mum had booked late notice (as people always seemed to).

I used the exterior of one of the uni buildings for a location, set up the shots, wore a fake smile the whole time and got the deposit and fifty percent up front. It wasn't ideal, but it would make a dent in the rent that month. So I happily obliged to some cheesy family shots as well as my usual package. I asked why they were doing it so far in advance of graduation. They explained that there's a chance the boy wouldn't graduate and also that his grandfather might expire before the real date, so they wanted some proper shots first. That was fucking tragic, but when I saw that old pops also had a furry yellow coating around his mouth, I completely understood and even gave them a ten percent discount. Poor bastards.

A text rang through from Leo.

LEO

> Some people are having a gathering tonight. Up in North End at the creepy house on London Road. You up for it? It's okay if not x

The last thing on my mind was socialising. Just spending a few hours out in town for work had wiped me out. I hadn't been sleeping. Couldn't remember the last time I actually woke up refreshed. I'd need a holiday or a coma to get some shuteye, but only one of those things was within my budget...

I messaged back:

> Okay. Just a couple of hours. I'm wiped.

— — — —

I looked through my wardrobe. It was obvious I needed new clothes. Everything was either too bright or too dull: T-shirts from uni emblazoned with funny quotes or memes, trousers a size too big or small for me, which I kept for no reason other than to remember the memories attached to them. Memorable hookups, events, moments in time. It was a sad state of affairs.

Jeans and a white tee it was. Whilst I showered, an email from Martina came through on my laptop. It had "URGENT" written in capitals in the subject line. I knew that reading it before I went out would just keep my mind occupied, but I couldn't resist a peek. As I opened it up, the battery went dead—the laptop was on it's last legs after dropping it in the kitchen. I didn't have the time nor patience to sit and wait for it to reboot. It would have to wait until later.

Out of either fear or distrust, I kept poking my head into the hallway, making sure I hadn't left the door on the latch (even though I checked four times), or that someone hadn't broken into my kitchen. The memory of the random stranger carving his insides right across the apartment was still on replay in my mind. I thought I might need some therapy when all this blew over. I'd seen too much dismembered flesh.

A taxi pulled up outside, and I slid into the backseat, rushing through small talk before settling back into the safety of my phone. With funny videos played on a loop, I tried to calm my head and avoid opening any emails or messages from the people I was ignoring. Bored, I refreshed the Portsmouth page on the forums a few times, but every post was a carbon copy of the one before it. Missing people… Acting strange. Drugs. Drink. Violence. The novelty was wearing off, and all the bad things were so commonplace they were becoming normal and day-to-day.

The driver had to say my name twice to wake me up. I'd fallen into a slight nap on the ten-minute journey. I thanked him and got out, climbing over the exterior metal gate to get to the front garden. I expected a few people to be out smoking or talking shit, but it was silent. A few lights were on at different places in the house—I could tell by the cast of orange seeping through cracks and corners.

At least if the party was shit, I had an excuse to leave early.

Something felt decidedly off. But it wasn't in my nature to listen to my intuition, so I carried on forward, momentum washing away any doubts and the screaming voice inside telling me to turn and sprint in a different direction.

Murmurs and whispers intwined with a heavy cloud of smoke as I pushed through the front door. The entranceway would have been grand and impressive if the building hadn't been condemned about three decades prior. The house had a sketchy history, but how it hadn't been knocked down and replaced with a block of flats or two was beyond me. Usually, developers would jump at the chance to make a few pitiful shared houses and a quick buck.

To the left, a large doorway branched into a living room, which was dimly lit by three or four table lamps spotted around the space. Murky brown wall-paper bled into tobacco-stained curtains and thread-bare sofas, currently occupied by four or five people my age or less. The rusty vintage bulbs gave every-one's skin a greasy, artificial hue, and their complete disinterest in my presence made the situation even more uncomfortable. To the right of the hallway the kitchen: piles of plates with caked-on rotten stains were stacked high in the sink. The wood panelling was chipped and gnawed by termites. I wouldn't be accepting any food or drink from these people. Not that the possibility of friendly hospitality seemed remotely likely anyway.

In that moment, I remembered the posts on the forums from that Bobby guy. *Go to the beach then come to the house.* I guessed this was the place he was referring to. I really shouldn't have come.

I filed straight through the hallway, past a young girl squirming on the floor, and right into the garden. Overgrown plants and dead grass framed the disappointing exterior, where three or four more people were hanging out. Leo was there. So was Cara.

My heart beat out my chest. They weren't kissing or laughing or even interacting much, but he'd made it quite clear that there was nothing between them. So why hadn't he answered my text or mentioned she'd be there? The time I was willing to spend at the party was dwindling with every new revelation.

"Leo. You're here."

He turned to me, dropping Cara like a bad habit. That made me smile.

With a big embrace and friendly squeeze on the shoulder, he offered me a drink. I asked if it had been anywhere near the kitchen and he promised that the only place it had been was in his backpack. I took a leap of faith and accepted a few swigs of the bottle. It was sour. A kind of pickled onion taste. Maybe he'd been eating crisps again.

Cara got the message and fucked off back inside, and I took out a pre-rolled cigarette, sucking hard before it was even completely lit. Leo looked at me, concerned. My gaze told him everything he needed to know. *It was just that kind of day*.

Things were awkward. I didn't have any words. Neither did he. We kind of hung there in the chilly night sky, both wishing there were other things to keep us entertained and engaged. There used to be a wealth of information on any topic that would get us going. Now, even the most interesting things were a sad pale grey. Leo hacked up a mouthful of sour phlegm, spat it out in the bushes. No wonder they were crispy and dead. I regretted taking sips of that alcohol before. The sour taste obviously wasn't pickled onion crisps. It was vile backwash.

"What's that?"

Leo jolted upwards, shifting from one foot to the other. In the shadowy garden, lit only by pale hints of moonlight, I noticed his pupils widen, crusty eyelids flickering as he took in an unknown sight in the distance.

"What's what?"

Slowly, he drew his finger up in front of him, pointing at a spot just above the horizon.

"That."

I heard a moderate buzzing, no louder than a fly when it hovers around a distant room in a silent house. Almost unidentifiable. But it obviously meant more to Leo. He ripped himself away from our conversation, bursting through the French doors with clumsy abandon.

"Come outside! NOW!"

I threw my expired cigarette onto the ground and stepped on the last embers to extinguish them. As the gaggle of party-goers spilled into the garden, I couldn't help but feel like I was the last one in on a joke. What the fuck was going on?

In a dreamlike haze, around thirty people stuck their hands up towards the same point on the horizon, gasping and shaking and mumbling nonsensically. Complete madness. One girl, dirty and covered in large pustules, turned to me, looked me right in the eye, and mouthed the words "You shouldn't be here."

Understatement of the year.

"Whose turn is it to try?"

The same girl, turning in an anxious rush. "Was it James? Raj?"

Like a gaggle of confused ducks, they muttered names in cycles until one of them had a flash of inspiration.

"It was Raj!"

A man stepped forward—claiming his name—and rushed into the kitchen. The others followed him.

"HURRY!" the girl screamed.

I wanted to leave. Needed to leave. But my curiosity had the better of me for the second time that evening.

Another randomer turned and flashed her rotten-brown toothy smile right at me.

"We're getting out of here. It's not too late for you."

"AHHHHHH!"

Spurts of blood shot at the glass doors: putrid streaks of pus and the darkest liquid crimson.

"Get him out!"

The sky erupted in streaks of white light, intermittent and fleeting. A rippling energy tore through the environment, subtle but disquieting.

Before my eyes could adjust back to the light of the house, Raj plunged through the opening, flanked by two random men. His entire outfit was soaked through with juices that belonged in his body. Eyes rolling back, a smile from ear to ear, he lifted his hand up high.

"I'M READY!"

The cacophony of sound reached fever pitch. I tried to control my breathing and think of five things just like you did in a panic attack but *oh fuck what in the Hell?*

Leo charged into me, knocking my shoulder, and I almost tumbled right to the ground. He didn't even notice. The sounds he was making. Feral. Violent. Ungodly.

Right in front of me, Pustule Girl reappeared, brandishing a huge blade.

Where the fuck did she get that?

She sliced Raj's abdomen. Carved away some epidermis until a flap of skin hung loose and floppy.

"Bring him back in! We need to get this right!" That was a voice from the inside, I think.

I followed the action this time. I needed answers.

I only just noticed the whole inside of the house was covered in a disgusting, yellow fuzz. The smell of damp hit me in between lingering metallic whiffs.

TEEEEEEAR.

"*AHKKKKHHH!*"

Raj had a tea towel between his teeth, clenching tight, the cloth threatening to give way to disgusting pressure. His eyes rolled back, gums struggling to retain control of his dirty yellow incisors. Pustule girl had a handful of loose skin, like a flesh version of the towel in Raj's mouth. Organs were on show. Red muscle slicked wet.

I stumbled back, found myself up against a cupboard. No-one saw me. Being invisible was good for once. I reached into my pocket, gripped my phone. With automatic reflex I scrolled to Dad's number. Sent a message. One word. "Help."

No reply.

Count five things you can see. Four things you can smell. Three things you can—

"FASTER! GET IT OFF!"

A disgusting slurp-sound as blades slid under flesh. Dark skin turned grey. Raj ran out of breath, but smiled still. A winning smile. Maybe the happiest he'd ever been.

Like old tapestry, the loose skin folded up as it was

being sliced away. Maybe someone could wear it as a suit when it was completely removed…

"That's enough. Before we lose them. Don't waste this chance!"

The group propped him up, dragged him through the kitchen to the back door. One man's job was just to hold the loose flesh falling from Raj's mutilated body.

Leo was back in the kitchen, looking on in ecstatic awe. He didn't even meet my gaze.

Raj was halfway across the garden—at the gate.

"It's your time now, Raj! Go make it happen."

High-pitched screaming. Raj stumbled out the gate. The rippling sound grew in volume and energy. It was almost physical, making its presence known, even inside the house. I slowly paced to the door and back into the garden. I needed answers. I kept telling myself that's the reason I was here. Part of me wanted to film this. A more realistic part of me knew that filming would just cause more trouble and unneeded attention. I mean, fuck, they'd skinned this guy Raj alive. But he was happy with that. What the fuck?

"They're overhead!"

"It's happening!"

"IT'S REAL!"

The whole scene was a haze. I had to stop myself from throwing up. There was so much blood everywhere. A complete crime scene.

Then suddenly—a roaring, industrial clang. A whoosh of wind. A battling clash of screaming voices. Then nothing.

"IT WORKED!"

I was already outside, halfway across the garden. I pushed through the back gate, past sweaty, clammy bodies that smelt of seawater and body odour. Bile rose in my throat. I felt it on my tongue, threatening to flood my cheeks and cascade out in a sickly waterfall.

On the floor in front of me, the remnants of Raj were scattered across tarmac, tiny segments of flesh burnt to the fence and brick wall. A sizzling, porky smell (that's it, bacon was forever off the cards), sickening yet maybe enticing in a way. A few metres ahead, flaps of scalp with scolded hair.

The group started to cheer. I needed to get away. Report this. Leave this fucking city. But I couldn't do that. I knew I wouldn't even have a chance. And if I thought any different before that moment, Leo's stare sealed the deal.

He pulled me to the side, hugged me in an embrace, trapping me within his arms. I'd never felt this unsafe or disgusted by someone I liked. Someone I loved. Everything about this moment was wrong. The smell of damp and copper in his sweat was overwhelming. I had to get away.

"Leo, I'm going home."

"No. Come with us. We need to show-"

I didn't let him finish his thought.

"I mean it. You're lucky I'm not heading right to the police station."

Pustule Girl stepped over, getting between him and I.

"You wouldn't want to. You don't know what's going on here. If you fucking—"

Cara resurfaced, dragging Pustule Girl away. A rotating door of weird Portsmouth characters.

"Take her inside. I'll see you at the pier," Leo ordered.

"Looks like someone's taken charge of these lot, then?" I remarked.

Leo snarled.

"We're all here together, Josh. We want you to be here too. Join us. Before it's too late. No-one's in charge, we're just ready. Getting ready together to leave this fucking place."

Sweat pooled at my brow. Leo kept on talking.

"Josh, you're not going to the police. You're not telling your Dad. Come to the pier. Everything makes so much more sense there. The videos didn't scratch the surface. There is *so much* more. Please come."

I stepped backwards. Leo stepped forwards. I wasn't going to let him win this one. When we were happy, I was always happy to admit defeat and let him take the lead. But not with this. Not after what I'd seen.

"I'm gonna stay with my Dad a while."

"No, Josh. You're coming to the pier. I can't spend another moment with you like *this.*"

"Like *what?* I'm not the one who's changed. I'm not the one running around with this bunch of degenerates,"

"Keep your voice down," he threatened.

I turned on my heel and started walking towards the door. Everyone's eyes tracked me step-by-step, willing me away with cautious optimism. Then fingers dug hard into my shoulder.

"JOSH!"

"WHAT?"

I span, pushed him away with open palms.

"What the fuck do you want?"

His eyes were severe. Hurt. Polluted.

"I just want my friend back," he croaked.

I stepped forward this time.

"Then get some help."

Moments later, I tried to retreat again, and Leo's hands were all over me. With a final warning completely ignored,

I pulled my arm back and punched him right in the nose. It splatted with a gross squelch, spurting snot and blood mixed in a phlegmy clot.

Completely betrayed, he did the same to me, sent me to the ground in a dizzying crumple. Eventually, I rose up, paced back to the front of the house and hailed a cab. A hundred metres or so up the road, when his silhouette had faded into the darkness, I started to weep. The driver didn't say a thing. My chest was tight. Eyes red raw.

And I still didn't have a message back from my Dad.

CHAPTER 17

At 10:00pm, I ate ramen at the kitchen counter. The locksmith was on his way, ready to make a tonne of money for the simplest of jobs. It was a last ditch decision, but I couldn't bear having Leo anywhere near me. He'd picked his side, become completely unhinged and took part in the killing (I think) of another person. I'd have to explain my actions to the police soon enough. And I'd be happy to tell my story.

The plan was to go and stay with family as soon as the sun was up, depending if anyone answered my cries for help. I'd deliver a key to Leo, post it through the letterbox of the creepy abandoned house, and tell him to collect his things whilst I was away. Then I'd delete every forum post, video, and scrap of memory I had with him. I'd start a new life in a new city with a newfound sense of purpose.

I cared for him deeply—too deeply—but there are certain events which transcend friendship, or whatever the fuck we were. Seeing him in that state, with those people, was one such event. And I wouldn't be dragged down with them.

For the rest of the night, I imagined what my Dad was up to, what kept him away from his phone for so long. He mentioned something secretive before, a job he was working on on the down-low. Whatever. I'm sure he was fine.

Then I spiraled, thinking of the night my Mum filled herself with pills as ten-year-old me sat and stared, intermittently watching cartoons. She gulped tablet after tablet, eventually succumbing to a frothy death at the climax of a show about lion families. It was so performative. So final. She wanted it burned in my memory, I was sure of it. She got her wish.

I remember her trying to explain her reasoning to me in extravagant detail: why she was ending things, what I should tell Dad, what I should do when her eyelids stopped fluttering, how to get to the phone if my fingertips didn't quite reach the handset. In those final moments, I felt bad for being so engrossed in the TV. It just felt so much more fulfilling than watching the end of such a fruitless existence.

Knock knock.

The locksmith steadied my shores. Stopped me spiraling.

I let him in, offered coffee, and watched as he twisted some screws and fitted a new lock. He was dragging it out —probably to mask how easy the job was in comparison to the price—and at the end of it all, I parted with a wad of headshot cash. It didn't feel as bad as I expected, though. The peace of mind was much more comforting. I could finally get a good night's sleep.

I needed rest. I'd been on the verge of applying for some jobs in different cities—Farnborough seemed promising—but had no energy or interest in it anymore.

Instead, I switched the TV on, flicked to some shit TV reruns about policemen driving around arresting people, and allowed myself to just marinate.

Thoughts came and went: fleeting emotions and reminders that there was a whirlwind of shit picking up speed around me, sirens buzzing in my mind like an early tornado warning. But I'd get to all of that. Right now, PC Jacobs needed to switch his sirens on to go and arrest an elderly thief at the pharmacy. My mind was so occupied with reality TV minutiae that I almost forgot Martina's email.

URGENT.

The word burned itself in my mind. I'd have to leave PC Jacobs to his crimefighting for now.

I opened my cracked laptop at the kitchen counter, plugged it in, and tapped my fingers whilst it rebooted. The email was waiting for me in my inbox, and I quickly opened it. Only a few words were in the body of the email:

Josh,

Think it's important to look at this. Water test results.
Let's meet up soon to talk.
Martina

That was it. I clicked on the attachment, and was pretty much dumbfounded at the contents. As confident as she must have been in her findings, I found ninety percent of it absolute gobbledygook. I'd need to meet her to translate it into something I understood. Maybe she knew that.

As I flipped my phone over on the counter to send her a message, I noticed three notifications. They were all messages from my Dad. Any initial relief I had quickly distorted into a grinding gurgle in my stomach.

DAD

What is it called. at the jjjgmdd. After it all. Dont state it or rate it no I can't.. Is it? Call back that is call right back boy.

Don't send help too late for that for me for you for Kat.

I re-read the messages about ten times each. Absolute nonsense. I dialled his number. No answer.

After being prompted to leave a message three times, I took the robotic voice up on its offer.

Dad. Not sure if you're drunk or whatever but I'm coming over first thing. Put the kettle on.

I tried to sound as calm and rational as possible. But something gnawed at my gut. Something was very wrong.

CHAPTER 18

I didn't like going to Dad's house. The area was nice enough, up and coming even. But for a policeman with so much pride in the work he did, he seemed to live in squalor. The front door was coated in a spray of dried-on dirt, probably from washing his car on the drive. Leading up to the house, overgrown weeds pushed through tight cracks in the paving. The front window had a deep crack in the upper left quadrant, begging to be replaced.

It's not like he didn't have the money to repair the place. It was more the time cost. Being a policeman was all he knew, and after getting home from a long day chasing criminals or shouting at young people or whatever the hell he did, DIY was way down the bottom of the list.

Usually, as I approached the house, I'd be able to see him in the window brewing tea, especially if I'd fore-warned him about a visit. I saw movement at the back of the house, silhouetted by the sun (the man really needed some privacy curtains too).

Knock knock.

"Dad. It's Josh."

I knocked the panel of the door. Then the letterbox. Then tried the bell.

Nothing.

"Dad?"

I rustled through my jeans for the spare key he'd given me a year or so back. I'd never needed to use it, but was silently glad I brought it anyway.

Inside, the smell of rotten meat wafted through the air. I felt burning in my nostrils and throat, and immediately covered my face with the inside of my arm. Soft footsteps gave way to a rattling mechanical sound. On full alert, I spread my back against the wall closest to me, and gently sidestepped towards the living area.

I didn't allow myself to move too quickly. If there was anyone else in the house, I had to make sure not to startle them. Whether they had good or bad intentions, starting off in a panic wouldn't do either of us any good.

"Hello?" I asked calmly, to no response. Something glistened near the back door. In the same controlled manner as before, I called out again. Nothing...

Until a blur of chrome crashed towards me, filling my vision in seconds. After the initial shock wore off, I saw it was one of the hazmats, like I'd seen at the beach and the tower block days before. They had some kind of cleaning apparatus in their backpack, but no sign of the bright orange hose that was quickly becoming their trademark in my mind.

"WAIT!"

I flopped back through the hallway, tripping over my feet to give chase. They were faster than I expected them to be in their heavy kit, but not fast enough. Before they had a chance to twist the front door handle, I careened into their back, knocking them flat to the floor.

"WAIT!" I begged, trying to get them to calm down. The person wriggled and fought, but didn't make any malicious attack. As their body stopped vibrating in fear, a tight knot formed in my throat.

The person behind the mask was elderly, probably nearing retirement. I'd just tackled an old person to the floor like a fucking rugby player. He probably had a broken hip or back or something.

Moments later, I helped him to the kitchen table, took off his mask, and made him coffee. I had a lot of questions, but the first one was an obvious one.

"Where is my Dad?"

He slowly shook his head, wrinkled neck skin pulling taut with each movement.

"Please. I haven't seen him in days," I urged.

The man shrugged, but didn't talk. He sipped coffee, intermittently looking over his shoulder for a way out. I'd been kind enough not to ask too many questions about why he was in my Dad's kitchen, but if he kept being so mysterious, I'd have to bring some heat. I was in no mood for fucking around.

"I really need to know where—"

The air felt humid. Overpowering. I felt my throat constrict as my mind tried to assess what had changed.

"I'm sorry. I really can't talk. My neck's on the line," he whispered, before standing up.

I didn't get a chance to reply. Instead, a dazzling white light burned through the apartment, searing my retinas and sending me to my knees. Two or three hazmats stormed the back door, spraying a plume of smoke directly at my face.

Fighting to stop my eyes watering, I clambered to my feet and started swinging my fists, attacking blank space in an attempt to connect with their bodies. It was futile, and though I landed one or two punches, it wasn't enough to stop them doing what they'd set out to do. Another dose of smoke from a different hose covered the surrounding area in a bubbly, slippy foam. My skin couldn't get a grip on anything around me.

The mysterious cleaners (a name I think fit their actions most clearly at that point) filed out of the house, packing their shit into a van. Like slick pop choreography, they slid into the vehicle and made haste without a missed step.

I, however, wasn't as graceful. After finally getting to my feet to unlock the front door, I fell head-over-ass out onto the paving and cracked my nose against the step. With a deep, exhausted sigh, I watched as the van made its escape, steaming down the road with no option to catch up to it.

"FUCK!"

There weren't many times I counted my lucky stars for the timing of events and near misses, but that moment turned out to be one of them. I stood, ready to start sprinting up the road, but with a millisecond of a second thought bubbling in my brain, I moved too late.

And thank God I did. Because just inches away from me, an ambulance barreled past my face, near enough grazing my potentially broken nose. The sirens wept as the vehicle sped to its destination, or as far as it was going to get... The vehicle took a hard left all of a sudden, and crashed into the side of a corner shop, crumpling on impact. I heard shattered glass and haunting screams, and maybe some putrid splashing of body liquids of some kind. One thing's for sure... I didn't want to stay and match the sounds to the grisly images.

"Where are they? Fucking. Skin on skin on skin! It fucking hurts you know!"

The voice came from my left… No. My right.

A skinny woman with half a shirt torn away stalked towards me from across the road, seething anger in her eyes and barely ten teeth in her mouth. I could see the blood from here, teeth torn from their roots and replaced with abscessed gums and probably an infection or two.

"I don't know you, lady!" I screamed, willing her to fuck off and give me some space. But she chose violence that day, and I wasn't prepared for the wave of anger inside my body to unleash so suddenly.

She gained on me, arms flailing, some kind of weapon bunched into a closed fist.

"You're not me! You're not us! You fucker! Fucking fuck you fucker!"

"I'm warning you!" I called out, begging her to stop so I didn't have to do something about it.

"Your skin is too taut anyway! Give me some and let's wear each other's flesh clothes!"

She had a blade… I knew it.

I wasn't going to go through this again.

When she was close enough to make contact with, I drew my fist back and launched it into her face with everything I had. She jolted backwards, nose popping. When I noticed she'd dropped the blade with the first impact, I rushed forward and head-butted her in the jaw, sending her into a pile on the road.

The plan was to help her up and apologise for my behaviour when she came around—I had never hit a girl before that situation. But the way society was getting more and more fucked up every second really clouded my judgement.

127

I reached out my hand to help her to her feet, but she ignored it, spitting a violent hurricane of vitriol my way. It didn't matter. Just seconds later, another ambulance sped into view, driving over her chest without a second thought or even a passing glance. Her crushed form convulsed on the road. I ripped myself out of my static panic and made a beeline for my car.

Key in the ignition. Gearstick in place. Reverse.

My car rumbled as I backed out of the space—I think to be honest I ran over the already flattened girl again, RIP—but I didn't look back. I couldn't. I kept my eyes laser focused on the road, watching for more emergency vehicles and people crossing the road haphazardly and more out of their mind, blade-brandishing psychos. This time, I wouldn't interact with them. It was too dangerous. Instead, I'd let my car do the talking, metal into flesh, and deal with any consequences later.

As my beaten-up vehicle drifted down the long road away from my Dad's place, I couldn't help but look around in disbelief. Things were bad. Really bad.

People were fighting. Arguing. Screaming. Emergency vehicles in every direction I looked. How had things got this bad? Why did no-one have any kind of answer to the shit plaguing this city?

Let's get this clear: Portsmouth has never been a happy little beachside resort. It's a grey, messy, dirty house of cards, ready to collapse at any moment from even the slightest nudge. But there were still charming bits in between, transitory moments where the sun was shining and people were dancing to music at a big outdoor festival, high on life and other narcotics.

But this? This was something else. Something mysterious and weird and downright alarming. People were sick. Really sick. And it wouldn't be long until things imploded, I was sure of it.

With one hand on the wheel, I grabbed my phone from my pocket, and called Martina.

"Hey, it's me. What's your address? We need to start working this out."

— — — —

F/ Portsmouth [latest]

u/victoryspecial [MOD]: Closing Threads.

Mod here. I'm closing any threads that talk about:

- *Disease*
- *Self harm*
- *Theories about the beach*

I'll open these up another time, but there are serious welfare issues at play here, and I think it's best that we keep discussions on this sub to more traditional points of interest. Food. Drink. Sports. That stuff.

It's only a temporary rule. I've locked this thread, so no discussions will be allowed. Anyone posting about the stuff above will be permanently banned from this page. Thank you for your understanding, and stay safe.

CHAPTER 19

Martina lived in a lovely detached apartment in Southsea, with its own driveway and everything. The rain was coming down hard, forming a mini whirlpool on my windscreen. The wipers battled what they could, but the last few minutes to her house were marred by near-misses and absolutely no visibility.

I parked on the drive, right behind a silver 4x4 that I recognised as hers. On the phone, she'd sounded concerned, almost unwilling to see me. It wasn't like her, so there was already a weird feeling growing in my stomach. All of the lights were on, aside from a room at the far side of the house.

Hiding myself from the downpour, I stood close to the door after knocking, trying to tuck myself under the tiny ledge above. Luckily, she answered and invited me in, with an offer of green tea or hot chocolate. I'm not a monster, so I picked hot chocolate. Things weren't bad enough for dirt water yet.

Drinks made, she sat opposite me in the kitchen, sipping on green tea with a face that leaned more towards grimace than inviting demeanour. Maybe she should have opted for hot chocolate too.

"Have you seen Tommy at all on your travels?" she asked.

I tried not to think too much of her son. Every time I did, I saw his dirty fingers pressing up against the gunk-filled abscesses in his skin. It was fucking creepy.

"I haven't," I answered honestly. "I'm actually taking a bit of distance from it all right now."

Martina nodded.

"Do you want some dinner?"

— — — —

Whilst a homemade stew bubbled away on the stove, Martina walked me to a small room at the back of her house. It was a makeshift lab, of sorts. She stressed that it wasn't up to all the standards and codes, and she wouldn't usually do any kind of important work in there. It was more for if she had a thought at night and needed to do a couple of quick tests to get her mind off things.

I don't know about most people, but if I can't sleep I watch TV or have a wank. To each their own, I guess.

The equipment in the room looked slick and efficient, but I didn't have a clue what any of it did. I recognised elements, things from TV and bad sci-fi shows, but most of it could have been alien technology for all I knew. Martina caught this, I think, because she explained in great detail what every step meant. Whilst she spoke and I watched intently, I noticed she had a print-out of the headshot I took for her in the corner, all framed and shit. That felt good.

"So basically. This water should not have most of these foreign bodies in it. Some of that is just the water network tainting the supply with literal shit. But there is one thing that's troubling me."

"Which is?" I asked.

"This."

Martina slid a small piece of glass under a microscope, and gestured towards it. I pushed my eye up against the malleable plastic, and closed the other one to get a good view.

Caught within the slide, some kind of organisms were moving and vibrating. I didn't know if it was a bacteria or virus or fungus, but it was unsightly. And not a great preparation for eating dinner at a stranger's house, I must say.

At the table, we discussed theories. I didn't have much input to offer, other than my experience with Leo, the campsite, and my cousin. Her ideas were a little more close to the mark, I think. Martina was fairly sure it was a fungus, and said that she was ninety-nine percent certain that nothing else like it existed in the world.

My mouth dropped at that. Gravy actually seeped out of my lips before I realised. After chewing it over (literally and figuratively), I reasoned that it couldn't be possible. No one person could know of every single fungus species in the world, plus there was a tonne of weird stuff we didn't know about the oceans and shit. It could have lain dormant all this time. But she was ready with a comeback, as I knew she would be.

Between sips of meaty gravy, cleaning her bowl, she explained that just two months before, she'd ran the same water test. And there hadn't been a single trace of this organism.

"It's natural, given the usual parameters. But *nothing* like this exists out there. That's the weird thing. It's like a brand new discovery."

My mind was full of information. I needed a moment.

"I need to go to the bathroom, which way is it, please?"

Martina took a moment, before gesturing to the back of the house.

"Last door on the left. Don't worry if you hear anything, it's just Daisy."

"Daisy?"

"My dog. Golden retriever. Lovely but ever so needy. Better to keep her out the way."

I smiled and sifted into the hallway, coasting through in a deliberately leisurely manner. I needed time to think. Time to work out what our next steps would be. What I could do to help Leo.

The bathroom was magnolia but fine. Tiled walls, cute seaside theme. Nothing out of the ordinary. I pissed and washed my face and patted myself dry with a slightly crusty blue towel. Back in the hallway, I followed the dim light back in the direction of the kitchen. Then I heard the first growl.

"Hello?" I whispered.

The door at the end of the hall vibrated on its hinges, first gently, then more violently. Thinking back to the exterior of the house, it was this room which had no light on. Martina mentioned the dog, but said it was a retriever. This seemed like a much more irritable breed.

More growling. I wanted to walk away, but felt guilty for getting the dog all worked up.

"Daisy. Daisy? Sssssh. Go to sleep."

I was going mad. Officially. Talking to a dog through the door.

I felt even more insane when I heard words start to spill out in wet gurgles. It wasn't a dog in there. It was very much human, which made this situation about a hundred times more sinister.

My brain told me to just go. Leave whoever the hell was in there alone and go back for more dinner. But a bigger part of me had mysteries on the brain, and it would have killed me to have another *what if* rattling around my head.

I checked over my shoulder to ensure I was alone, then reached for the lock, taking the clasp in my fingers. Gently, I lifted and drew the metal bolt to the left. With an open palm, I pressed against the wooden door and let it creak open. I inched forwards into complete darkness. I couldn't even see three metres ahead of me.

Hesitantly, I reached for my phone and switched on the torch. The beam cut through the black, illuminating a narrow section of the room as I moved the device left to right. And then I saw it.

"Fucking cunt get me out!"

I stumbled back out of the room, gulping a deep breath of air. My phone fell screen-down, the torch light casting the area in a soft glow.

I could see Martina's son Tommy chained to a metal bed frame, soaked in his own piss and shit and God knows what else. Everything in the room had been packed over to the very perimeter, presumably to stop him grabbing anything sharp or dangerous. I heard the footsteps behind me at a severe delay. Martina was already arching over me, slamming the door shut and bolting it back up, before I could place the sound.

"I didn't want him to hurt himself."

She crouched down to my level and picked up my phone for me.

"I think there's a way we can fix this," she sighed.

— — — —

Back in the lab room, I had my phone back, and Martina didn't seem pissed off. That was a relief, but I still had my guard up. People don't think rationally when their families are in danger, and I didn't want to walk into any other awkward situations. I had enough on my plate.

She mentioned that the fungus would have some kind of *kryptonite*, for lack of a better word, a natural anti-fungal or some kind of weakness against existing pharmaceuticals. There were a few places to start, but time was not on our side.

I offered my help, but she politely declined. I'd decline any scientific help from a photography grad too, to be fair. We weren't any closer to helping those we loved, but at least it gave a little bit of context to our situation.

After another helping of dinner and a glass of wine to top it off, I thanked Martina for her hospitality, apologised for sneaking around her house, and promised that if there was anything I could do to help, I was just on the other end of the phone. It felt good to be doing something helpful, and if it could help cure our friends and family, I'd go to any lengths to make it happen. On the way out, she mentioned that she really did have a dog called Daisy before, and showed me the decorative box she kept her ashes in. A weird move, but I understand why she did it.

As I stepped outside of the house, a notification rang up on my phone screen. It was Mani.

MANI

Can we meet? It's about Kasey.

Same place as usual. 9am tomorrow?

MANI

Can't you meet now?

I left that message unanswered. I really wish I hadn't.

CHAPTER 20

On top of the concrete building, we were at the complete mercy of the weather. The rain was just a drizzle when I first got there at 8:58am. By 9:03am, it was torrential. Mani had rushed straight into the conversation, without any greeting or niceties.

"Kasey's dead," he said, deadpan. And before I had a chance to react, he continued, "And it's all my fault."

"What do you mean? How?"

"She said she wanted it, Josh. That everyone was talking about it and she didn't want to be left out."

"Mani, what the fuck are you saying?"

He took a deep breath. Blinked a few times.

"I took her to the beach, Josh. Took her into the water."

Usually, there would be plenty of questions to follow such a vague statement. But with the amount of shit happening down by the water, it was tragically obvious. Mani explained a few more things, obviously hoping for me to connect or sympathise or something like that, but I found my eyes drifting to his mouth and eyelids. I don't know how I didn't spot it before.

Yellow fungal spores were just about visible, branching from the place you get that crusty dust after sleep, sneaking from his lips like a sickly yellow cold sore.

So far, it seemed like you had to have direct contact with the water to get infected. I'd been around several people with the disease—Dad, Leo, Tommy—and didn't have any symptoms yet. Leo fell in the water. Dad mentioned he'd been in it, and Tommy, well, that's where we found him to start with. Swimming in the sea was off the cards for a long time.

"How long since you went in?" I asked bluntly.

"Two days. And I don't think I can deal with this at all."

"What does it feel like? What is it?"

Mani shook his head.

"I try not to think about it. It makes my brain hurt and then I get all isolated and weird."

As he lifted his hands to scratch his face, I noticed wounds traced up and down his arms.

"You did that to yourself?"

"I don't want to talk about it."

I rolled my eyes. I'd brought a stack of scrap papers to make aeroplanes, as if the childish pastime would help bring back happier memories or give me something to do with my hands. Instead, they were soaked through, the delicate fibres melted into a gloopy mess in my backpack.

"Why didn't you tell me before? Why didn't you talk to me before you went in? You knew I was investigating it," I pressed.

"Because trying to get your attention feels like sending a DM to a celebrity, Josh. You haven't been there for us since Leo moved in."

"Sorry," I said. "I know I've been distant."

"You're not sorry," Mani said. He wasn't wrong.

I sighed. Looked around the skyline. Grey on grey on grey. Of course.

"I think I might do it as well," Mani said.

I was too busy thinking about Leo and my Dad to hear him the first time.

"Where did she die, Mani?"

As he opened his mouth to talk, I felt my phone vibrate. Being the shit friend I am, I raised my hand to shush him—we could talk about suicide after my call. When I saw the name on the screen, I swiped right away.

INCOMING CALL: "Dad"

"Dad?"

Robotic static. My Dad's voice, distorted, mangled.

The call ended. Only the essence of words, nothing I could understand.

"That was your Dad? Is he okay?" Mani asked, but his voice took up space that I needed to use for thinking. When he spoke, it was like an annoying child trying to get your attention when you're working and you've already said no to playing three times already. His droning was a mere vibration somewhere else.

The call didn't return. I stared at my phone again, willing it to give me an answer or a clue or something in between. I tried to redial several times, but it wouldn't connect. Fucking typical.

By the time I looked back up at Mani, ready to continue the conversation, he was already mounting the guard rail. Without a second look back, he sighed apathetically, and flopped forwards off of the building.

I heard the crash, splatter, and screams below. I didn't bother looking—I'd seen enough of the inside of people's bodies recently. Enough to last a lifetime, in fact. I heard the sirens first, and then the clattering of the rooftop door just after. Two policemen approached carefully, making sure I didn't plan to follow Mani to a bloody end. Then they pinned me to the ground like I was a criminal or something.

The rest was hazy. I explained what happened in my own words, agreed to a written statement, and then finally got a chance to ask my own questions.

"Do you know my Dad? Have you seen him recently? Some weird people were inside his house."

Without any response or acknowledgement, I was stuffed into the back of a police car, driven to the station, and dropped outside hours later with a stomach full of coffee and not much else.

"Can we take you home?" an officer with a scratchy-looking beard asked.

I declined. I didn't want to be at my apartment. In fact, I didn't want to be anywhere at all in particular. The only thing that felt right, the only hint of something that could be described as a plan, was getting Leo away from those people. Whatever *this* was had overcome him, and the more I saw how people inflicted with this… illness… reacted, the more I knew my days with him were numbered.

Martina was supposedly working on finding a cure. But it wasn't enough. There were too many days between now and "someday". I wanted him back with me. Then I'd get us far away from here. He should never have moved to Portsmouth, if he'd have just stayed put we would be virtual friends living it up in cyberspace. Instead, everything had gone to pot. I wasn't going to let this city tear us apart.

— — — —

F/ Portsmouthengland [latest]

u/rashidamoans [MOD]: Started a new sub. Free to talk about ANYTHING Portsmouth on this page [fuck those other fascists trying to censor us on F/Portsmouth]

=

So I'll start. Who else thinks this whole thing is a military stunt gone wrong? Rumours about lights under the water. Some kind of biological weapon making people crazy. I'd love to see any other theories…

-

—> **u/ *justinreynolds1***

Covid jabs. How many times do we have to tell you sheeple?!

-

——> **u/ *jon_underscore_name***

It's too much of a delayed reaction to be the Covid jabs you idiot. Next you'll be blaming the 5G towers. We all know what is really is.

-

———> **u/ *justinreynolds1***

Yeah? And what's that smartass?

-

————> **u/ *jon_underscore_name***

Those foreigners coming over on small boats. Brought some kind of foreign lurgy over ain't they.

CHAPTER 21

The early evening sun hung in the sky, looking out of place and kind of surreal. It was freezing cold, dingy and dull outside. The sun was set dressing at this point.

I parked a few roads down from the London Road house, aware that my last visit had been a whole nightmarish situation of its own. I didn't want to bring uncalled attention to myself right away. If I could just knock the door, speak to Leo, and get him to come with me, I'd be able to formulate the rest of the plan in the car. There was no way of knowing he was definitely there, but intuition said he probably was. I'd try listening to it this time.

There was the chance, of course, that he wouldn't come, that his weird crew of fucked-up friends would jump out and beat the living daylights out of me. I didn't pay too much attention to that scenario. I decided to put some positive thoughts out into the atmosphere. The narrator of the self-help audiobook I abandoned would be proud of me.

Taking a leisurely walk up the path (deciding whether

or not this was the right course of action), I stopped just inches short of the imposing, rotten door. If I put my ear against the wood, I could probably gauge how many people were in there, how safe it would be to interrupt them again after a less than friendly exit last time. But I didn't want any weird insects to crawl into my ear canal, so I decided to just go for it.

Two loud knocks. I was already talking myself out of it. Too late, though. Someone answered in just a few seconds. It wasn't Leo. It wasn't Cara. It was the brown-toothed bitch from before.

"What?"

"I need to talk to Leo."

"We don't go by names here."

"Well, what do you go by?" I asked, playing along.

She shook her head, tutting in disgust.

"What the fuck do you want?"

The smell from inside wafted towards me, assaulting my nostrils like a wave of putrid manure. I couldn't help but cough, snatching my head to the side to avoid fully vomiting on the girl.

"It's okay," a voice from inside spoke. "He's here for me."

Leo.

But when the man I expected walked to the door, it was like a stranger had taken his name and voice. Pale, skeletal face. No T-shirt, just contoured skin and ribs trying to break free. His usually soft hair was greased behind his ears, missing clumps, a DIY haircut gone wrong. His face was pretty free of the spores, but the rest of his body was covered in crispy lemon scabs and deep orange skin lacerations. Fresh tears and red-hot grazes peppered his body.

I remembered how it felt to hold him close, his breath in my ear as we vibrated as one. How intimate and sexy and *real* that all felt. This didn't feel real. This was a nightmare masquerading as reality, a peek into some parallel universe where everything I loved was rotting and spiteful. I didn't recognise the man in front of me.

"You coming?" he asked, leaving the door open but unbothered as to whether I followed or not.

"Is there anywhere we can talk?" I asked the back of his head, trying to catch up with his rapid pace. He led me into the kitchen, waving away a couple of snot-covered teens to give us a private moment.

"What is it?"

I took a moment. I had everything planned out in my head, but seeing him in that state with all of his light dimmed and spark extinguished was impossible to contend with. Finally, I mustered up some words.

"Can we go home? Talk this over?"

Leo snarled, his lips twisting into blistered flaps.

"I *am* home."

"No. You're not. We live in the apartment. We have ramen on Thursdays. We *talk* about things that are on our mind."

Leo didn't speak for a moment. Then he howled with laughter.

"Fucker. Last time I saw you, you punched me in the fucking face."

"You punched me too! You wouldn't take no for a fucking answer."

"And what are you doing now, huh Josh? No hard feelings. None at all. Okay? I thought we had something, but it was just a little friendship that went by the wayside. So let's just fucking leave it there should we?"

The smell was even worse in the kitchen. I couldn't get my mind off of it. Even whilst Leo talked, the dirty, bittersweet notes stung my nostrils.

"Okay, Leo. So what the *fuck* are you doing here? Hanging around drinking and smoking and doing drugs? What about your job? What about your ambitions?"

He laughed again, taking a moment to hack phlegm onto the kitchen floor.

"Well Joshy, I quit the fucking arcade, and there's more to life than dreams and ambitions and shit. I'm not a dreamer like you, head in the clouds. Fucking... I don't have my little degree to fall back on and snap pictures for spare change... People. Taking fucking... I don't have a Dad to pay half my rent."

That hurt. Pins and needles in my chest.

He was slurring. Just like the others, his sentences were getting mixed up. Blunt. Short. Nonsensical...

"What? Why are you being weird about this?" I asked. "He pays for half of both of our rent. You're off your fucking head."

Leo pulled my neck, dragging my face close to his.

"Listen to me. You don't know what's coming. Up there. Down here. You don't know what's going on, not like we do. You could have gone to the beach... the fucking beach with us. We'd have let you in. Told you everything."

"You're sick, Leo. You need antibiotics or something for those wounds."

"Oh fuck off, Josh!"

He pushed me hard, slamming me into one of the kitchen chairs. I decided to stay seated.

"This," he spat, rubbing the skin on his arms, "is

nothing but a coating. A raincoat for the real *us*. A way to get in up there… do you understand?"

It's safe to say I didn't.

"What you don't get," he continued, "is that we aren't going to be here much longer. So forget about me. Forget about all of us in here, and go and live your life. Okay?"

Leo stormed out, already at full-speed by the end of his sentence. I followed him into the living room, recalling the sight of the murky brown wallpaper and tobacco-stained curtains.

I didn't see it initially. I was too busy stewing in my own anger to even give context to the sight in front of me. Cara's sarcastic doe eyes were staring right at me from a spot on the mantelpiece.

Her head was completely detached, slopped above the fireplace like a Christmas ornament or a hunting trophy. My stomach twisted; I tried to vomit. There wasn't anything left to bring up. As I raised my head, I saw body parts scattered around the space. Arms and feet and scraps of skin. But in the middle of the room, the focus of at least five people's attention, was a mutilated body. Cut off at the neck, with all limbs removed, and deep crevices erupting from the flesh.

These demented fuckers were taking turns poking their fingers deep within the tissue, licking them clean and going in for a taste with their tongues. Obsessed with flesh whilst simultaneously treating it like the most common-place thing ever. I couldn't stop staring. Blood stained almost every surface.

"Is that…?"

Leo smiled, unzipping his jeans.

"Cara's? It is. And don't worry, she videotaped her consent. She knew sacrifice was the important thing. We're one. You don't get it. She'll get taken up another way. This flesh we all wear is just for fun. She gifted it to us until we meet again later."

With the end of a screwdriver, he reopened a gaping, crusted-over wound on the corpse, set right around where the belly button should have been. In this state, it was just a mutilated body with no arms or legs or much anything else—a scrawny, rectangular slab of flesh.

My vision blurred. It was like I'd been thrown into one of the old torture porn movies Leo and I used to watch on Saturday nights. The flesh had to be just a prop, the house a set drenched in buckets of blood and filled with jump scares and mutilated bodies; at the end, things would turn out okay, and we'd enjoy a nice, safe sleep afterwards.

Leo pulled his underwear down and stroked his limp dick until it got big. He spat a glob of milky phlegm onto his hand and massaged his meat. He watched as the other people in the room helped themselves to different holes in the flesh plaything, poking until bodily juices seeped from the wounds, dripping onto the carpet in stringy globules. Leo stared, sweat dripping from his forehead, as he got off to the horrific scene.

To a chorus of squelchy groans and grunts, Leo came in his hand, and circled away from the corpse.

"Hey Josh?" he asked.

I was unmoving, silent in my spot.

Then, he flicked his hand forcefully in my direction, covering my face and clothing in his lukewarm spunk.

"Get the fuck out of here."

Tears started to pool in my eyes. I wiped the sticky residue away from my face, and tried to calm myself down.

"He liked it before, everyone! I don't know why he's being so shy!" Leo taunted.

I couldn't handle it anymore. I turned around, sprinted to the door and cranked the handle to the left, forcing it open. Wiping down my clothes as I left, I didn't dare turn back.

It was over. It was obvious to Leo. Obvious to everyone there. And now to me.

The roads leading to my car blurred into one long grey walk. I got into the vehicle, twisted the key in the ignition, and just drove. Without any particular destination in mind, I circled the streets in North End, watching as people stumbled around with no real direction. I wondered if they were unwell too, or just a casualty of this city and the people in it. In some ways, I envied how pointless and depressed they looked, without any kind of care or worry in the world.

In my own selfish mind, I imagined exactly what they were thinking: where their next drug fix would come from or where was best to shoplift in the early evening, the places without security guards or fancy CCTV. It was a horrible stereotype to tar these people with, but my positive thinking had all but gone out the window, and I felt trapped in a cycle of despair and anger. I could smell the putrid, dried-in semen in my shirt and hair, and wanted nothing more than a shower and a good night's sleep.

I stopped driving around in circles, and decided to start on the route home. Somehow, I ended up on the hill with a burger and milkshake, and several curious stares directed my way. After filling my belly with fatty beef and oily chips, I was ready to face home and the blank abyss where my best friend should have been.

On the way back, I tried contacting Martina, my Dad,

and then Mani (even though I'd seen him jump from a tower block—I think I was in shock), cycling through the many people that seemed to be ignoring me at the moment.

No-one picked up.

CHAPTER 22

I met with my Uncle Bob the next day. He said there'd been some updates about Kat's death, and that he wanted to talk to me about it. I don't know why he couldn't speak to his wife or any of his friends about these things—we barely knew each other—but I guess with my Dad out the picture for now, I was one of the only close family members left.

At around eleven thirty in the morning, I drove over to Fareham, a town just outside of Portsmouth. Similar vibes, but on a smaller scale. All the good and bad bits from the city, just distilled into a tighter space.

Bob's choice of meeting place was a chain pub on the high street. Not my usual haunt, but I decided to humour him because I couldn't think of anywhere better. Bob was a bit of a lad, to lack a better term, and I couldn't see him settling into a quaint café or coffee shop. Two pints ordered, we sat at a booth in the corner.

"So you've really not heard from him?"

I shook my head.

"I had a couple of weird text messages. But he didn't

send me any money this month for the rent. And he wasn't at his house."

I left out the bit about the mysterious strangers at his place. That wouldn't help clear anything up.

"Why's he sending you money to help with the rent? You're a man now, Josh. Need to get a good job and a girlfriend. Start growing up."

Bob had just lost his daughter. That's the only reason I didn't bring up the fact that he continued to fake several injuries to stay on benefits, despite being more than able to sell dodgy cars for cash in hand, and go to the gym three times a week.

"What news did you get?"

His face changed from usual apathetic middle-aged man to something more solemn.

"They found more of Kat. Stuck up a tree. Bits of skin and organs."

Gross.

"Apparently some birds had been nesting in her leftovers."

Well that was fucking charming. Bring me to the pub in the morning on an empty stomach, make me drink a pint of warm beer, and then bring up leftover flesh.

"And they still have no idea how it happened?"

Bob shrugged.

"Why would her body parts be up a tree? It doesn't make sense."

"There was another thing I wanted to ask. Your Aunt Shelly—sorry, just Shelly—she does her early morning cold swims over at Hotwalls, doesn't she?"

Hotwalls was an area down Old Portsmouth, known for being quite upmarket and bougie. Mostly residential, with a café and a small pebble beach tucked between old structures.

"She does? I didn't know."

"Yeah, has done for ages. She's always posting about it on Facebook."

That's why I had no idea. I blocked the bitch after her constant anti-vax memes and distrust of anyone non-white or British.

"Well, I've been hearing that the water… Something's up with it."

I took a deep breath. I could just about deal with all the death and weird goings on inside the city, but if my Aunt was going to be making an appearance, poking her fingers into crevices or skinning herself in the garden of that old decaying house, I think that would cross the line into satire. My life would officially be one big joke. Wake me up and get me breakfast, because I'm nightmaring.

"Is she displaying any symptoms?" I asked.

"Symptoms? No. No, I don't think so."

"Then I think she'll be fine. But maybe she could lay off the swimming for a bit… just in case."

After washing down the pint of beer (which got warmer from all the chit-chat) with a sour grimace, I said my goodbyes and ambled back to my car. I had another reason for popping in to see Bob—I was on the way to a headshot booking up in Birmingham. It was a bit of a drive, but I planned to stay overnight in a hotel, and get a bit of R&R to wake up fresh the next day. As well as a chance to kick back and chill out in a different place, it was well worth the price I'd floated (and the client had accepted).

I hadn't talked to the client much but they seemed friendly over messages and dropped a deposit to cover my travel up to the hotel. To be honest, I'd have offered to waive the rest of my fee just to get out of Portsmouth for a bit, but there was rent to think about.

On the sliproad out of Fareham, I got a horrible knot in my stomach, a twisting ache that screamed *something is wrong* and that I should probably turn back and stay put just in case. But I didn't. I ignored my body's gurgling wails and cranked my speed up to eighty miles-an-hour to get the fuck away from this place.

— — — —

F/ Portsmouthengland [latest]
   u/oblongtextures:
I'm going to the beach. My little girl had trouble in the water yesterday, when her Mum took her for a dip. Nothing happened, as far as I know, but they've both been acting weird since. I discovered all the threads on here about the beach this morning, and I'm horrified that the council aren't talking about it? With our water company pumping ten tonnes of shit and sewage into the sea every year, is it any surprise that people are starting to get unwell? I'll leave an update if I find anything. I'm talking to my local MP on the phone tomorrow.

   -

   —> u/ *staywithmememe*
   Any updates OP? Did you find anything there?

   -

   — —> u/ *abacusfacewash*
   Uh-oh.

CHAPTER 23

The drive to Birmingham was fine. The motorway was clear. I stopped a couple of times for a coffee, piss, and a sandwich (not in that order) and arrived at my destination just before 4:00pm. I'd booked a chain hotel room, first floor, so I didn't have to heave my equipment up too many flights of stairs (because of course the lifts were out of order). And you can get fucked if you think I'm leaving my camera case out in my car. Not in this place.

As I rolled the hard case through the narrow hallway, I could hear a mish-mash of what I liked to call "hotel noise": screaming kids, rattling bed-frames, rushed hoovering, and loud sneezing. Luckily for me, there was a little section at the end of the hallway separated by a glass door where three or four "luxury" rooms were located. They weren't really luxury, just a step up from bog standard, but I wanted the soft sheets and big bath and an extra divide between me and the holidaymakers. I was here on business, you see.

I hung up my clothes, had a shower and a wank (in that order), and charged my camera batteries. I'd arranged to meet the client at a swanky Korean place in the city, which meant a taxi journey or a bus in a couple of hours. I used the time in between to rest, watch TV, and flick through some of my old images as inspiration.

This client, Jemima, was a wannabe actress, had a nondescript Southern English accent, and pronounced her S's with a weird lisp. She'd moved up to Birmingham to find theatre work because "London wasn't for her" and found my profile on an old casting website. Whatever. She was paying me just short of a grand so I couldn't care less about who she was or where she lived or anything like that. I napped until my alarm.

— — — —

I waited at a table in the window for half an hour before ordering a Kimchi pancake and bottle of peach soju. I'd finished both before I felt a buzzing on my phone. No sign of Jemima -- it was a text from Martina.

"Can I call you?"

I downed a tiny shot glass of soju, then took a big swig from the bottle. After the sour fizzing in my gullet levelled out, I called Martina.

"Hey, Martina. I'm just waiting on a client for a meeting but thought I'd give you a call instead. How are you?"

"Josh… Uh, not good actually."

I asked her why.

"I got all my results back, from our tests? There's nothing we can do at this stage. I've tried antifungals, natural medicines, experimental medicines I shouldn't even have access to… But… It's Tommy."

"What happened?"

There was a long pause. I silently ushered the waitress over, paid, and left the building whilst waiting for a reply.

"He's gone. Not gone, gone, but… he escaped. Broke the chain. I think he's back with Leo and everyone."

I sighed hard. Even hundreds of miles away from that shitstorm I couldn't relax.

"I'm in Birmingham. I have a shoot tomorrow but will be back in the evening. I can help you then."

"No, no. I'm going to get him now… Wait. You're in Birmingham?"

I explained the situation, and then asked why she sounded so shocked about that.

"You must not have seen the video. I was wondering why I couldn't see you there."

CHAPTER 24

I couldn't breathe. My body was red hot, sweaty, itchy, irritated. As I stood in the doorway of my hotel room, jaw slack, knees shaking, I felt as if I could just destroy everything around me. But I wouldn't, because I didn't have the money to lose my deposit and hoped that I could still get an ounce of peace in this place tonight.

For the third time, I swiped the video off-screen, and tried to call Leo. He wasn't answering. Of course he wasn't.

Because he was streaming live from my (our) flat, the busted front door in the background of the shot, swarms of his fucking putrid new friend group spread across the space doing God knows what. Some were smoking. A couple were shaving each other's heads with my beard trimmer. My bedroom door was wide open, and people were rooting through my stuff.

I couldn't handle this. I was hundreds of miles away. Even if I got into my car now, sped home as fast as I could, what then? There was no way I'd be able to get them all out of the house. I called the police and was assured that someone would "check it out", but that news was delivered in the same tone they promised me they'd find my bike when it was stolen two years ago off the street. Spoiler alert, they never fucking came round. I didn't speak to my Dad for two weeks after that, until he bought me a new one as a peace offering.

As soon as the ringing cut out, I called again. On the live video, I could quite literally hear my call coming through on Leo's side. But he just snarled, ignoring it until it rang out. Martina explained that she'd go over and have a word, especially because Tommy was in one of the rooms ODing on some kind of drug by the looks of it.

I bet they were smoking all my weed too…

And then it clicked. I had to get through the doorway and sit on the edge of the hotel bed to absorb this realisation.

I'd been set up.

In the background of Leo's livestream video, one of the dirty, unwashed fungus-carriers was screaming along to some music on her phone. And in between her massacre of contemporary pop hits, she described what was coming next to no-one in particular. *Her voice was pretty nondescript… Southern English accent…She had a lisp when she tried to pronounce her S's….* They'd set me up with a fake meeting to get me out the way.

"FUCK!" I screamed out loud, joining the cacophony of "hotel noise" I'd tried so hard to separate myself from. For anyone in the hallways, I was just another weird person in a hotel room. Maybe I would never be more than that.

I watched Leo's livestream in disgust. At this point, it just felt like an out of body experience, me lingering on the bed, unmoving, a statue with a phone in its hand.

"Coming to you LIVE from my apartment. My flatmate's

out but that's fine because he's not my mate anymore and he doesn't even know what's coming. For anyone that does, and has been to the beach and through the initiation and knows exactly what's at stake here, I need you to listen to me very carefully. People on socials, on the forums, fucking SHEEPLE... they think we're unwell. That we're infected. They don't understand that this is the end. You've seen things out there. You've come face to face with the ships up above. Hell, we all want to get to the next level, but our ambitions don't come true here on Earth. They come true UP THERE. So join me. Make your sacrifice and make it count because things are about to get really fucked up down here. Anyone who stands in our way will be dealt with: if that's police, neighbours, parents... we've all decided what we want, so leave us the fuck alone... And, Josh?"

My heart raced at the mention of my name. I heard the door knock behind him. One of his friend's went to open it... Martina was at the door.

"What happens next is all your fucking fault."

The video froze.

LIVESTREAM ENDED.

— — — —

I took a bath.

A warm foam of bubbles encased me, protecting me from the outside world. It was like a soft, temporary coffin; it made me think that maybe death wasn't that scary. I set the tap to run as hot as possible, so the air steamed up and my skin flushed red, and I felt slightly dizzy and out of my mind. On one level, it was like trying to remove the toxins from inside of me, drown the shit that had seeped deep

159

into my skin (talking conceptually, of course). But in reality, I just felt a bit sick and faint. Bath-time was over.

As I dried off, I couldn't help but let my mind wander to the forums. I knew people would be speaking about Leo, and I needed to know what they were saying. How much sway did I really have to get back the apartment and end this once and for all?

Instead, I was met with a text message from *him*. It was a video link. I clicked it.

His face appeared in close-up: acne-ridden skin in 4k. His eyes were milky, glazed over. For a moment, he just fucked around on the phone, trying to test the settings or something. Then he smiled, yellowed teeth covered in furry fuzz.

"Joshy boy I told you this would happen!"

The phone tracked across the ceiling, then a quick hint of the floor, as if a child was trying to record their first video. But then the frame landed on Tommy, who looked about ten times worse than I'd seen him before, all locked up at Martina's house. His face was covered in blood and dirt, as well as the trademark abscesses, which had now taken on a sickly, gangrenous texture.

Leo's voice came from off-camera.

"Say hi, Tommy!"

Tommy smiled. Snarled. Gave a sickly wave. Then the frame span back to Leo. It was a dizzying experience to watch.

"Before we show you what happened just now, I wanted to check: you were there when your Mum killed herself right? You got to see all the last moments in glorious detail? All alive, high as shit, and then dead? Well, you'll be glad to hear that Tommy was afforded the same experience…"

The sick feeling in my stomach returned. I really

should have listened to my instinct and stayed in Portsmouth.

"Are you ready, Tommy?"

And then the camera swung back round to Tommy, who had Martina's lifeless head in his hands, gripping her silver-grey hair in clumps to get purchase. I dropped the phone, but couldn't tear my eyes away when it fell face up.

The camera tracked down to the body, which was surrounded by the feral group that tagged along with Leo. His voice appeared from behind the phone camera again.

"We're taking some pieces of her as a memento. She can't come with us now, but she's part of the bigger picture. Just like Cara was. A way for us to practice before we make the sacrifice with our own bodies."

They were carving slices out of her body, taking chunks with scissors, keeping flesh fragments as a good-luck charm of sorts. Cackling. Howling with laughter. Her own son, desecrating the corpse of his mother. My sickness transitioned to anger, a jolt of rage surging through my body.

With Martina gone, I was back to square one.

Within minutes, I'd packed my case, left my keycard at reception, and got into my car. I called to let the police know what was happening, and that I'd be sending them a video when I stopped at the next service station. I was hell-bent on revenge; for Martina, for me, and for what Leo and I could have been. Away from this city. Away from this Hell.

But, no more.

I compressed the accelerator, swerved in and out of traffic, slowing only for the speed cameras. Then right back to it. I ignored my bladder, ignored my shaky hands (on the account of a lack of caffeine). I didn't even stop for the heavenly four cheese panini at the service station. Stomach rumbling, eyes tired, I was on a mission.

And I'd only stop when I had Leo in my grasp. I didn't know how it would end, but I wasn't going to allow him to destroy my life. He'd already taken so much from me, so much time, so much energy, so much space in my brain and heart. This next step felt final. The start of the end.

Blurred landscapes shot past the windscreen, streaming fog-lights oscillating and refracting on my wing mirror. My fingers were gripped tight around the steering wheel, body bent forward, as if my posture would get me there that little bit faster.

Then, a thought passed through my head for the first time, like a train thundering through a station.

To stop Leo, I might have to kill him.

That thought would have destroyed me before.

But right then, in that moment, I didn't feel destroyed. I felt determined. Red hot and ready to burst.

— — — —

F/ makeuptipsuk [latest]
u/lashlovelife: MAKEUP HELP!

I need help with my skin. I've been using a new brand of eyelash glue, and I have this weird coating around my eye and underneath my eyelid [picture attached]. Does anyone know what it might be? It started at the eye, but I have patches around my mouth, in my armpit and groin.

-

—> u/ ashkaspellbound

Go to the doctor, our advice can't replace a doctor visit. That said, it looks maybe fungal? Is it a popular brand?

-

u/ *lashlovelife*

I did get it from a discount store online but it's the real deal. I've attached an image of the product too.

-

—> u/ *ashkaspellbound*

Hmm. Definitely weird. Go to the doctor to get it properly checked babe x

-

u/ *lashlovelife*

Will do. Thanks x

-

— —> u/ *jeezelouise321123*

Have you been on holiday recently? Particularly in Hampshire/ Portsmouth? Any swimming?

-

u/ *lashlovelife*

My dad lives in Portsmouth, so just a dip at the beach. Why??

CHAPTER 25

I don't think I took a deep breath the whole way home. My anger was breaking through, my facade slipping.

Parked outside my flat, I recalled one of the first dead bodies I saw in the city. The young guy had been spread across the very road in which my car idled right now, body streaked across tarmac like red jelly.

I could see them all in my living room and bedroom. The balcony blind was open, so I could see straight in from the road. As I slipped out of the driver's seat, I tried to plan my next steps. There was option one: go in all guns blazing, smack the shit out of as many of them as possible, and see where that got me. But I'd seen how easily they carved up Cara and Martina, so what would stop them from gutting me like a fish?

Option two was smarter. Knock the door, ask to speak to Leo in a calm and controlled manner out the front... And then smack the shit out of him one-on-one.

Every one of my plans ended with me fighting Leo. It probably wasn't a viable option, not with his gang of gangrenous goblins, and not given that for some stupid reason I really didn't want to hurt him.

Before I'd even picked an option, I was at the front door. The lock was broken clean off, so the door was kind of hanging shut, without being locked.

Knock or push...

Push.

I swung open the door, looked around, trying to spot Leo in the sea of putrid features. The smell was hazardous, and it would be safe to say that any safety deposit I hoped to get back from this rental was well and truly lost in the caked shit-stains and vomit-marks. There was shit all over the walls, puddles of puke and piss and sweat and semen.

"LEO?"

The blur of flesh and bodily liquid concealed him. I was too focused on the strangers lounging around my house, injecting and snorting and giving blowjobs and half-assed hickeys to one another in a truly deformed *last hurrah* of human life.

I tried to shout his name again. Before I could form the two syllables, a frying pan collided with my head with a heavy back swing.

Black. I was breathing still. But my head was ringing. I think my eardrums burst. Did my eyeballs pop? No. I was still hearing. Still seeing. Fuck, my head. Time to sleep.

CHAPTER 26

Leo woke me with a glass of lukewarm water to the face. I immediately fought to get my bearings. I was tied up, on a chair, in his room. It used to be decorated with band posters and polaroids, but they were all on the floor now, in tatters just like the man he used to be.

"Leo, let me go."

He was pacing around the room, looking all kinds of crazy. Despite the rotting external shell he currently inhabited, he actually looked more put together than the last time I'd seen him. Maybe he'd had a shower? Sorted his hair out? I don't know, I was looking at him with double vision and a headache that screamed *just cut your head off, who the fuck needs a brain anyway?*

"Leo?"

"I'm not letting you go. Shut up."

"Charming," I said under my breath, confused at how calm I sounded.

"Listen to me, Josh. Fuck. I need to know why you've left me to do all this shit by myself?"

"You fucking what?"

Clarity came quick, like a slap in the face. With a hand though, not a frying pan.

"It wasn't my fault I fell into the water. You should have come after me. Then all of *this* wouldn't be so fucking difficult!"

I shook my head. Not for long though. I could feel my brain moving.

Leo leant against the wall opposite, staring right at me. He had a knife. I didn't realise that before.

"You gonna kill me with that knife, Leo?"

He looked down at it, then shook his head.

"Nah," Leo muttered. "In my head, it seemed quite like, I dunno... romantic? Like I'd kill you and then myself, and maybe things would all be okay as we were back in this house together and perhaps when we got to heaven or hell or whatever, we wouldn't remember the last few weeks? We could tell ourselves it was an overdose or some shit and just carry on as we were."

I giggled at that. He really was off his head.

"But then I thought: fuck. I've gone *all* this way, done so much shit, and I don't even get rewarded at the end? What the fuck kinda fair would that be?"

My mouth was dry. Really fucking dry. I wanted to ask for water (in my mouth this time, not across my face), but knowing him he'd probably bottle up some beach juice to try and get me all infected and on his wavelength.

"Can I get some milk?"

"No," Leo said. "Not right now. I'm talking."

Motherfucker.

"Here's what's happening. In an hour, I'm taking you down the beach. Police are round, so gotta be careful."

"I'm not going," I said defiantly.

"I'm not giving you a choice this time. No, no. I've been doing this shit on my own long enough."

I rolled my eyes.

"And then, we're gonna bait them. Get them to come to us, and track right back to their base."

"Who?"

I quite literally had no idea what he was talking about.

"The ship. You saw it so don't say you didn't, fucker. At the party. Raj got taken up."

"Taken up?"

Leo grabbed a glass from his side table and launched it at the wall. It shattered and sprayed everywhere. It reminded me how thirsty I was again.

"You're *infuriating!* Copying what I say, not listening, telling me that you're not doing anything I fucking say. Well guess what? You fucking *are* and we're going to the fucking beach. And then we're tracking them back to their base so we can get on board and stop living this *fucking shitty life in this absolute fucking God-forsaken hellhole!"*

"You're insane! Actually one hundred percent need-to-be-sectioned insane, Leo. You think whatever those things in the sky are... are what? *Aliens? God on a flying go-kart?* Just what do you think is happening here?"

Leo got close up to me. His breath stank.

"Whatever is in the water has opened my eyes, Josh. Our eyes. We just need to give our body as a sacrifice. Just like you saw Raj do. They're coming to save us. Taking pity on this place, on this race. They're going to take us up and let us live a new life without any of this shit."

I didn't even have words.

"Rahul out there has access to CCTV across the city from his job. We have intel. A whole fucking system to find out where these ships are going and coming. All we need to do is bait one, get them to take one of us up with the tracker, then we're set. We'll go after them and force the fuckers to take up every one of us. All of us, Josh. Including you."

I sighed. I couldn't work out if my head hurt more or less after hearing this plan.

"Sorry, mate. I don't have *going to space* on my bucket list."

He backhanded me right across the cheek. My neck cracked. It weirdly solved a lot of my pain. And then, after a moment of indecision, he dropped the knife and curled his hands around my throat, squeezing hard.

I fought against the restraints, rope burning the flesh on my wrists and ankles. The headache came straight back as I started fighting for each tiny breath. His face blurred. A heavy black dot appeared in the middle of my vision. The veins popped in Leo's exposed arms. I think I saw tears in his eyes but it might have just been that weird milky liquid.

As I felt myself slipping away, my last memory on Earth Leo and his grabby hands, he let go. He screamed at himself in infected gibberish, smacked his head off the wall like a child in a tantrum, and grabbed the knife.

His stare felt like a million sharp needles.

"Fuck it. We're going right now."

CHAPTER 27

Two young men around my age stuffed me into the back of a Land Rover that smelled distinctly like cat's piss. Not human piss. Cat. That's what I tried to persuade myself, anyway.

I didn't bother asking where we were going a third time. The first couple of attempts had been met with a kind of smug apathy. They knew precisely what part of the beach we were going to, but I wasn't going to know. That kind of thing. I wouldn't have a chance to formulate an escape plan.

The roads were peppered with police blockades and a swarm of emergency workers. It's like they suddenly decided to pay attention about a week and a half too late. I tried to get a glimpse of every face through the window as we sped past, hoping one of them would be my Dad. No luck. Whoever was driving knew a way around the blockades. We were coasting right through. Perhaps they really did have some kind of intel.

The driver parked the car in Old Portsmouth, just next

to the pub at the far corner. A small, walled-off area sat at the end of the road, custom-built to give old people a place to sit and eat chips with an uninterrupted sea view. A central concrete platform was set in the middle, with smaller seating areas peppered around the perimeter. The square, as it was known, was empty right now, and it seemed the perfect place to conduct whatever plan was about to go down.

Leo came and knocked on the window. The driver took a deep breath, grinned into the rearview mirror (I could see yellow fuzz in his teeth in the reflection), and hopped out the car. He popped his head back in before he shut himself out.

"See you up there."

And with that, he flashed a grin at Leo, nodded whilst they talked about something I couldn't overhear, and went on his way, stalking over to the central reservation. He stepped up, and just as he did so, the door by me opened.

"Come out and watch this."

I didn't bother arguing with him this time.

Just like the old days.

The chilly air brushed against my cheeks, stealing any warmth I'd built up in the car. The driver was now talking gibberish up at the sky, wielding a small multi-tool with the blade outstretched.

"We need to get back. They only come if we sacrifice alone," Leo explained.

I didn't bother asking what that meant. The others got out of the car, and retreated behind us. Leo and I snuck round the corner, using the pub as cover.

The driver punctured his arm with the blade, twisting it to create a meaty gash, hacking at the flesh that still connected his wrist to his forearm. Before I knew it, the concrete beneath him was dirty crimson, and his body shuddered in a way that told me he'd be on his knees in seconds. The idiot had cut one of his main arteries.

"Watch this," Leo whispered in anticipation.

It was impossible to tear my eyes away from it, frankly, and after a few seconds, the man did exactly as I thought. He fell to his knees, strength giving way. I wasn't sure what I was meant to be seeing, but it was nothing out of the ordinary.

"Is this it?"

Leo looked at me, bloodshot eyes rolling.

"What do you think?"

The air around us dropped, a strange temperature change of sorts. I'd only ever felt this once before, when Leo and I first saw the weird shape in the sky, before the madman outside became streaky sauce on the tarmac.

"What's going on?" I asked, almost sure I was being pranked.

The driver started gargling, screaming, head craned up towards the sky as if he was shit-talking God himself.

"It's here fucking knew it fuck this skin fuck this suit I'm gonna be up there looking down up there waiting for you all!"

The others started howling. Clapping. Chanting. He carried on slicing and blabbering. It's almost like the act of self-harm took them into some kind of weird trance.

"What's going on here?"

"New eyes new skin new face new body new mind new heart new fuckstick new asshole," the driver continued.

"LEO! TELL ME WHAT THE FUCK IS—"

WHOOOOOSH.

A bright light burnt through the late afternoon sky, intermittent, white-hot, pulsing. Ripples of energy threaded through the air, as everything in the immediate area started to drag upwards. The driver's hair looked as if it was being pulled by an invisible string, all of his clothes and loose skin flapping up like gravity had reversed.

"Gonna be a new me now you won't believe it fuckers! Take my skin take my sacrifice have it all you can drink the juicy juice of my old flesh and use my limbs as whatever the fuck just take me up take me up TAKE ME UP!"

He transitioned from this nonsense talk to a gut-wrenching roar as his skin started to separate from the muscle and bone, the impossible force tugging upward. A deep mechanical crunch whirred in the atmosphere whilst a shadow formed over the walled-off area.

I looked up and almost puked.

I couldn't identify the flying vehicle. Matte black, interspersed with silver plating and frosted glass panels. A reservation in the centre with some kind of deadly-looking fan revolving at a million miles an hour. It was hovering right above the driver in some kind of hellish *fuck you* to everything I knew about science and the world I lived in.

"How the—?"

The screams got louder. The driver was pulled from his knees to his feet, hovering midair for a moment whilst he unravelled his legs.

"See you up there!" Leo screamed, his voice breaking.

And just like that, some of the driver went up, and some of him stayed down.

His head detached furiously, spine fragments clattering to the ground. Most of the skin and clothes from his upper body peeled away, de-gloved. A blood-curdling cacophony of crunching and soft tissue slapping together filled the air as intestines and lungs were snatched by the sky, whilst his stomach and genitals slopped to the floor.

Time stopped. The scene in front of me was hyper-visceral. Too much to take. My mind wandered, looking for any way out. I studied the brickwork pattern on the floor, inhaled the smokey chemical scent that lingered behind, wondered what other weird things it smelled like: bleach and BBQ and athlete's foot cream when you've been walking round in thick socks and boots all day.

I wanted to talk, wanted to question every little thing I just saw, but my mouth wasn't ready. To my side, Leo was clapping, joined by the other cronies that had come along for the ride. With a flick of his greasy hair and a knowing look, he mouthed something to me.

"Told you."

What was I meant to think? I'd pretty much seen evidence of some kind of flying saucer right in front of my eyes. But there had to be another explanation. In fact, I demanded one. Everything up until now had been within the realms of possibility: weird fungus from the depths of the ocean combined with mass hysteria and a social media-induced panic of unprecedented scale. This, however, defied explanation.

My head hurt. Bad.

Leo paced over towards me, cutting a much softer figure than he had the past couple of weeks. His eyes were tired but persistent. I knew exactly what he was going to say, even before he said it. That's the beauty of knowing someone on a level deeper than most do. You can read their expressions. Their tics. Even their innermost thoughts and desires—just from a look. Even when they were this beaten down by some kind of virus. Even when the world around you is on fire and crumbling to the ground, it doesn't take away the very human skill of connection and empathy.

"We need to go to the water now," Leo muttered. "With any luck, the tracker got sucked up with the rest of him. So we go to the water... then we track this vehicle. End this all today."

And for the first time since this whole shitstorm started, I didn't have a good enough reason to say no. I had to think for a moment. All of these people seemed *certain* that going into the water and giving some kind of sacrifice was the key to getting taken up. And being taken up—even in such a violent, deformed manner—was apparently a good thing. The start of a new life. Beyond this present. Beyond this flesh-bag we live in.

I wanted to believe it more than anything. It would solve every issue I had:

I don't have a steady pay-check—doesn't matter, you're off to a new life in a new world.

My Dad has disappeared and won't answer anyone's calls—doesn't matter, you're off to a new life in a new world. Maybe he's there too!

I can't find a boy who loves me for who I really am—you get the picture. He's right in front of me, desperate to take me up with him and hopefully spend some kind of eternity up there.

The amalgam of burned flesh and charred clothes right in front of me wasn't filling me with hope, however. Leo seemed to clock this, as he kept moving to stand right in front of my field of vision.

"I'm scared," I told him, the brutal truth.

"I know. But we're here. We'll help you."

I looked to the floor. Looked back up at him.

"But we have to go now," he continued. "This is our big moment. We can't wait a single millisecond longer."

— — — —

F/ Portsmouthengland [latest]
u/Joshx4265ab

I'm writing this as a final note, just in case any of my friends or remaining family come looking for me. I think I've got everything wrong. I'm writing this from a car, on the way to the beach. There are police everywhere, it's not an easy journey. They've already stopped us once. It was a close call. But I wanted to admit that I was wrong before whatever is going to happen happens. I want to apologise to Martina and Mani and Casey and Kat and my Uncle Bob and Shelly etc (still not calling you Aunty, get over it).

Things have been really fucked up for a long, long time, but I think it's worth giving up my one-man fight, and just giving this thing a chance. I'm outnumbered and saw something today that really changed my mind. It's weird how that happens.

I want everyone to form their own opinion on this. Lots of you have already been to the water. Lots of you are thinking about it. I'm not here to tell you yes or no - you can disregard the videos I made previously, as I didn't have any evidence. My goal isn't to sway you one way or another. Just give you the cold, hard facts as I see them.

I saw one of the vehicles today. It feels ridiculous and stupid to describe it as a ship, but from what I saw, it's the only real thing I can compare it to. It hovered above us, and sucked this guy right up from the ground. It left bits of him behind, just like what happened to my cousin and other people from some anec-

dotes on here. That was the thing I needed to see to make my mind up. I hope each and every one of you get some clarity and personal evidence before you go to the beach. I also hope that I see you all again someday, in a place that is a bit less hellish and dystopian than Portsmouth. Cheers to that (*clink*).

CHAPTER 28

I'd only meant to close my eyes for a second. By the time the car stopped, I'd been asleep for almost ten minutes. It took that long to get to a part of the beach that wasn't swarmed by emergency services.

Every ten seconds or so, I could see some kind of struggle outside the window. Police officers fought with disturbed, fungus-infected fanatics. Cars crashed into each other in a desperate frenzy, trying to get out of Southsea and the city as a whole. Bins were on fire. One guy had a machete, hacking off bits of him and others in savage, random swipes. He didn't even look infected. Just an opportunist with an opportunity to see some blood and cause some mayhem.

I'd expected the whole beach to have been cordoned off by now, but whenever barriers had started to be erected, there were plenty of people fighting to break them down.

Leo was in the driving seat this time. The two vehicles in our mini convoy were playing musical chairs, given that each of the eight (well, seven now) people kept switching cars. Maybe it was just coincidence. But I suspected it was more the fact that this was personal for Leo. He wanted to make sure I got in the water without issue.

The cars pulled up in a small off-road car park, which was meant to be locked up but had been carelessly left without a padlock. We all filtered out onto the road, keeping to the inside so we could avoid getting caught by the police. I don't think they could figure out what was happening—it's not like I was an unwilling participant in this any more—but Leo said we were better safe than sorry.

I felt the crunch of pebbles underfoot as we ambled towards the coast. I thought of days at the beach as a kid, my first kiss over by the pier as a teenager, mine and Leo's ill-fated camping trip to Hayling Island and the old man rotting on the grass. The water had always been such a common, everyday sight I'd never had a chance to really study it, to look at the waves and ripples and how its colour was really sickly and odd. Soon, I'd be sucking up the putrid green whilst my whole body was held underneath.

Before getting in, I asked if I could take my shoes and socks off. It was a simple enough request, albeit strange, and it was granted—if I could stop stalling and just get the fuck in. Leo's words, not mine.

Seaweed caressed the webbing of my toes, slimy stems rubbing greasily against tender skin. The rocks felt prickly in the water, not soft or smooth. My jeans soaked through immediately, clinging to my legs as if warning me to step back. The water was up to my hips now, and Leo was stalking right behind me, his spindly fingers digging into my right shoulder as we walked. The sky was painted burnt orange, the last hints of daylight fading out.

"It hurts a little bit to start with," he whispered.

"Whilst your lungs fill up and your feet can't touch the floor any more. But then it's like a wash of relief. It all opens up to you, the knowledge of this place. Just wait and see."

It was up to my chest now. My t-shirt was plastered tight to my body, collarbones poking through.

"That's far enough," Leo warned. One of the others tried to approach, but Leo waved them off.

"This is between me and him."

Leo paddled towards me, grabbed my hair softly. I could have sworn he was caressing me, considering me. But any glint in his eye quickly disappeared. Back to business.

"Ready?" he asked, as if expecting an enthusiastic 'yes'.

He gripped tighter, started to apply pressure to my head. I felt my knees start to buckle, my posture flexing into a crouch.

"This it it, Josh. You'll be with us. With me. Finally."

BANG.

A gunshot.

Leo lurched back from me, releasing my hair. I tracked the horizon, searching for the shooter. And then I saw a police officer with a handgun pointed towards the sky. It was a warning shot.

Another officer hopped into position, a megaphone in hand.

"Get out of the water."

"NO! GET AWAY FROM US!" Leo screamed at him.

Before another warning shot could be fired, Leo lunged towards me, but I instinctively pulled myself to the side, letting him tumble into the water. A sickly gargle escaped his throat as he went under momentarily. When his head surfaced, his eyes were black. Unforgiving.

"LEO!" a girl called from the shoreline. "We just had a hit on the tracker! We need to go!"

"WE'RE NOT DONE HERE YET!" he screamed at them. And then, at me: "YOU ALWAYS HAVE TO FUCK THINGS UP!"

The girl paced, shaking her head.

"We need to go *now!* It's our final chance."

One of the officers tried to grab her, and that launched the other five friends into a manic attack. They knocked the officers to the ground, disarmed them, and pulled them by their legs into the sea. Moments later, they were soaked through, heads underwater, fungus filling their lungs as they thrashed and fought not to drown. The girl grabbed the handgun, checked the chamber like she knew what she was doing, and slid it down the back of her shorts. Hopefully, she'd had the forethought to click the safety on.

Leo came at me again, but I slapped his body out of the way. He laughed, chanted at the sky.

And then, almost silently, defeated: "You don't even deserve to be up there with us. I'm done."

He turned, swimming towards the shoreline. But he wasn't done with me yet. Infected or not, I wasn't going to be let off without doing my part.

"Get over here or I'll get Kelsey to shoot your cowardly ass."

I did what I was told, my cowardly ass shivering as I swam back towards the shore.

"Where is it?" Leo asked as he surfaced.

Leo and Kelsey talked a bit, though I blocked it out. I wanted to escape, or maybe just go back into the water and drown, I wasn't sure anymore. Why was I so resistant to joining them? If all was to be believed, it would be more of a miracle cure than an actual ailment. But something deep in my gut was begging me to wait it out. Let all this blow over. I listened to my instincts for once.

I heard the police officers fight their way to shore. Sirens erupted in the distance, threatening an influx of backup and the prospect of being outnumbered. We rushed forwards, tracking our way back to the vehicles. I almost made a run for it, a last-ditch attempt for freedom. But I didn't dare. If I was caught this time, Leo would just have killed me.

— — — —

I'd been relegated to the other car now, where there was no Leo. But there was Kelsey with the gun and a fat guy I think might have been called Oscar. His face was greasy and pitted, but it looked like that had been a long-time affliction, not a fungus thing. Neither of them really spoke —just ground their teeth together back and forth, babbling nonsense under their breath. But every now and then, Leo's voice would come through on speakerphone, and they'd spring into action, talking about tracking devices and speed and the easiest way to find out where the ship was going to land.

"You're gonna regret not getting dunked," Oscar said. The sirens in the distance reminded me of the impending danger, but no-one else seemed to care.

"You'll be left to all this shit whilst we eat lobster in paradise," Kelsey followed up.

I almost reminded her that you could get all-you-can-eat lobster down the road without having to be ripped into a million shreds before you had the pleasure, but I thought I'd better keep that to myself. I wanted to get out of this alive, not die at the hands of these two.

"We're headed towards Portsdown Hill. It's starting to slow down," I heard Kelsey squeal excitedly. Then they both went back to silence and their twitching eyes, pained utterances, and spaced-out ways. One of them opened a window, which only wafted their stench right back into my face.

Imagine not showering for a week. Multiply that by ten, roll around in some shit, and then mix it with some chronic damp. That was half as bad as it really was.

I was counting down the moments until I could make a run for it and be free of these people forever.

— — — —

F/ Portsmouthengland [latest]
u/LE02019xyk

IT'S TIME. For everyone who's part of the plan, follow the tracking information. If you don't know what I'm talking about, you're not meant to, so fuck off and enjoy dying here in this Godforsaken hellhole.

CHAPTER 29

I heard the revving first. Then, in the corner of my eye, a group of beaten up cars merged onto the road. Each vehicle was packed to the brim with people, a variety of ages and backgrounds.

The police presence was as heavy as ever, but we were building in number. My gut flipped, nervous energy bubbling near my bladder. I could have easily pissed myself without affecting the smell in the car, but I was already uncomfortably moist, so I decided I had to hold it.

The four-lane road quickly transitioned into two lanes, then a roundabout. Coming off of that, I could see Portsdown Hill in the distance: an imposing chalk ridge, as wide as the city and then some, rising hundreds of metres above sea level.

"Where now?" Kelsey questioned, waiting for direction from Leo.

A blur of forest and trees swept by as we accelerated uphill. Oscar cocked a handgun, looked at me with a yellow grin through the rearview mirror.

Leo's voice erupted through speakerphone. "All the

way up until you get to the inn. Take a left. We're going through the fort."

"That's crazy," I piped up, uninvited. "Surely there'll be a tonne of police there?"

It was Kelsey's turn to look at me in the rearview this time. One by one, I saw her slowly lift her fingers off of the steering wheel. The car jerked, choked, begged for direction.

"What are you doing?" I screamed.

"Things are with a higher power now. Let it be."

We veered dangerously close to the edge, and I almost unbuckled my seatbelt to grab the wheel myself. But after a throaty cackle, she grabbed it, corrected course, and carried on.

The vehicle whipped round the corner, sped across a long stretch of road, and jerked right to take the turning for the fort. A police cordon was spread ahead, and we slowed to a halt, waiting for several other vehicles to join us in a queue.

They'd been expecting us. This road led right from the beach to the fort. Of course it would make sense to set up a blockade, especially with the trouble we'd been causing.

"GET OUT OF YOUR VEHICLES," one of the officers screamed through a megaphone. They were right in front of us, lit by giant floodlights on the other side of the wall.

"3…." Kelsey counted.

"WE WILL SHOOT. TURN AROUND NOW!"

"2…"

A minibus pulled up right behind us.

"Don't forget to come get me, okay?" Oscar asked her. Before she replied, he opened the door, slowly rising to his feet with the gun above his head, as if surrendering.

"1…"

"PUT THE WEAPON DOWN,".

The door clunked shut. And then Oscar sprinted to the right, aimed his weapon, and started emptying rounds into the officers. Megaphone Officer fell back with a gunshot wound to the face. The others started firing at Oscar, automatic weapons spitting out tonnes of white-hot shells onto the road.

I ducked down as Kelsey put her foot on the pedal, bursting towards the cordon. She mowed down the first three officers with ease. Bodies crumpled under the tyres, bones snapping and flesh mashing. From somewhere out of my eye-line, she grabbed her own small gun, firing haphazardly out of the window.

Seconds later, her head was blown out with a hole I could quite literally see through, blood splattering back onto me. My jacket was covered in her brain matter, like little udon noodle fragments begging to be slurped up with ramen. Kelsey's lifeless body in the driver's seat shielded me from the bullets pelting our vehicle.

We started to lose momentum, until the minibus rammed from behind, driving the vehicle forward with reckless abandon.

Gunshots blew through the metalwork, only just missing my face. I was still crouched behind the seats, ducking down as much as I could. Before I knew it, we made impact with the front gate, which thankfully hung loosely open and not locked shut.

A ripple of energy swarmed the atmosphere as a ship passed overhead. I don't know if it was the one we'd been following, or if there were several of these things, but it gave the convoy a newfound excitement.

The driverless car veered into a wall, blocking me from

opening the door. I was trapped. Outside, I could hear gunshots and crunching glass, screams and frenzied attacks. I had no idea where the group had got their guns —maybe a police officer or gang member or whatever— but it seemed as if they were picking up and attempting to use the dead officer's weapons too.

The back windscreen shattered, shards of glass raining down on me. A dirty hand presented itself, and I grabbed it. With a heavy heave, the hand dragged me through the back of the car, and onto the floor behind it.

Leo.

He didn't wait for me. There were many others with him. Twenty or so people ran in a crowd, heading across the large grass expanse towards a destination I wasn't clued in on. Bright searchlights brushed the perimeter as the crowd stormed, burning through the impending darkness.

The Portsmouth skyline was visible above the mounds of raised ground that spanned the perimeter, small tunnel entrances peppered every twenty feet or so along with various out-buildings and towers with no discernible features. I was lost, and started to think I should have paid more attention to their ramblings or maybe just gone under the fucking water.

Automatic weapons rattled as bodies collapsed to the floor. I didn't dare try to follow the crowd. Instead, I scoured the brickwork around me, saw a door, and slammed through it.

With momentum, I careened into a dark brick room, nearly tumbling down a rickety spiral staircase. I remembered reading about the tunnels under the forts in Portsmouth with little more than a passing interest. There were several forts on the hill, built to protect the city in the 1800s. I had no idea what they were used for nowadays, but I didn't have our own miniature version of Area 51 on the cards.

I grabbed my phone from my pocket, switched on the torch, and cursed under my breath when I saw my battery was at 43%. Minding my step, I used my hand to guide me around the twisting walls. For a moment, I just listened. For footsteps or the cocking of a gun or some kind of supernatural sounds I related with '80s B-movies.

A long, dusty brick hallway presented itself in front of me, lit by a dim festoon of work lights. From my position, I couldn't hear any of the ruckus from above ground, but vibrations from the weapons and maybe an explosion of some kind vibrated through the brickwork. Beaten-up metal doors lined each side of the hallway, with small chalkboards etched with information about the contents of each room. I rattled each of the handles in turn, but none of them opened. According to the scribbled chalk writing, they were just storage anyway.

I paced towards the end of the hallway, where there was a final, mysterious room. The door was cracked open, a cool chill filtering out onto my skin. A rack of metal shelves stood in the middle of the space, which had rounded walls and a thick layer of dust covering just about everything. Sunlight beamed through the barred windows, exposing thin strips of rusty machinery and miscellaneous documents strewn across the floor. I almost left, rethinking my plan, until I saw a shoe in the corner.

On closer inspection, it wasn't just a shoe, but a foot and a leg and maybe a whole body, shrouded by a blue tarpaulin. My gut rumbled again, reminding me that I should have eaten and still needed to empty my bladder. But it also felt like an instinct, a warning, a suggestion that I shouldn't look under the tarp, and just leave things as they were. I could plead innocence, grab some white material to wave like a flag of surrender... It wasn't too late.

Against better judgement, I reached forward and snatched the material back.

Oh God, no.

I recoiled, choking back bile that had seeped into my throat. Eventually, I just let it dribble out, dry heaving and thankful there was nothing to bring up.

I wasn't ready to let this sight be real. Staring, I just studied the form, begging my eyes to adjust and show me something else. Something normal. A mannequin, or a blow up doll, or something else that definitely didn't belong here.

My Dad's body. Deformed and bloody and broken. Flies buzzed around his rotting skin, fungus peeking out from his nostrils and what was left of his jellied eyes. But it wasn't the fungus that had taken him. Two gunshots had left entry wounds in his neck and chest. Sticky, coagulated blood lay in every crevice and wrinkle, lump and bump.

Despite the blood and thick carpet of dust, I sat next to him. I grabbed his hand, leaned in for an embrace. Silently, I said sorry for being a shit son and blaming him for Mum's overdose and not letting him win me back. I said sorry for taking his money and relying on his help instead of helping him a bit. No tears came—weird, right?—but I was sad and bubbling and maximum grey.

More than that, however, I was angry. Angry at whoever did this. Angry at this city for letting this happen. Angry at myself for not noticing all the clues around me.

As I let him go, I felt something hidden behind his back. I tugged, first gently and then harder, until his police notebook revealed itself. The cover was bloodstained, as were the edges of the paper, but after a quick flick through, I saw the main writing was still legible.

He said he'd been investigating something. Something secret and huge, which would blow up when it was revealed. This was it.

Dad wasn't the kind of man to stay silent. He pushed and prodded and poked until he got answers, and this had obviously been his downfall.

How did he get in? Under what pretence?

I opened the notebook, and started looking through the scribbled handwriting.

— — — —

POLICE NOTEBOOK - BOOK 4 - Portsmouth

- *First night - woman at beach (Jade). Boyfriend (unknown) missing. Turns up dead on shore. Jade questioned. Released. Fungal infection?*
- *Second night. Disturbance Old Portsmouth. Old woman (unknown). Naked, knocking on doors at midnight. Self-harm wounds. Lost sight of her. Didn't hear anything else.*
- *Third day - unknown aircraft. Showed up by police station. Another sighting at beach. Third sighting in Cosham (near Portsdown). Kat?*

- *Third night - disturbance at beach. Kids. Paramedics called. One of them dies from knife wounds. Self-inflicted.*

Rest of these notes occur various dates. Can't remember exact order:

- *Couple arguing at beach. Both have weapons. We chase them into water. I trip. Submerged.*
- *My son Josh and housemate (Leo) at beach. Residents in water. Situation between them and Josh / Leo. Leo gets dragged under. Submerged. Paramedics called. All okay. I drop them off.*
- *Aircraft seen again. Two sightings. One sighting - old man, 65, unknown name - says that person underneath was "pulled apart" by energy wave. Followed up. He didn't want to talk about it any further.*
- *Get a tip off from Fred. Works at Lifelong Corp. Government subcontractor. Vehicles are part of a new top secret rollout. Gives me the below information:*

1. *VEHICLES are ASCA's (Autonomous Specimen Carrying Aircraft)*
2. *VEHICLES transport, retrieve and dump scientific specimens*
3. *GOVERNMENT are aware of a dangerous spillage at Portsea beach. Toxic chemicals dumped from ASCA in mid-2023.*
4. *GOVERNMENT working on top-secret containment mission. Need to destroy all samples of the spillage, and anyone infected with it*

5. *PUBLIC are reporting 'sightings' of UFOs. GOVERNMENT and SUBCONTRACTOR are happy for this to continue, and pass all off as a conspiracy after containment mission complete.*

6. *Top secret documents will be made public in due course by whistleblower. Estimate around two weeks from when I speak to him.*

CHAPTER 30

I stared at the notepad for ages. The handwriting was rushed but legible. If it was true—which was far more likely than the alternative—I needed to stop this suicide mission right now. This group needed a hospital, not a distorted pipe dream about aliens and planets and having dinner on Mars with fucking Dr. Zoidberg.

The festoon lighting in the hallway flickered out, replaced by a coruscating blue-red emergency beam. A deafening siren rang out from hidden speakers, ripping through the space and vibrating off of the walls.

I grabbed my Dad's wrist—tried to heave him up and drag him with me— but it was futile. I promised to come back for him under my breath, and give him a proper, respectful burial. Then I grabbed the only item in the room that could be remotely helpful as a weapon: a mallet from the metal racking.

As I peeked around the corner back into the hall, I was relieved to see it still empty and safe to pass through. I could have sworn I heard Leo calling my name, but at this point, I couldn't even trust my senses. I sped through the space, past the beaten metal doors and dusty alcoves, and ascended the steps in a practiced pattern.

Near the top, I could hear screaming and shooting still. If I could get hold of a gun, there was a small chance I'd know how to use it. I used to love learning about that shit when I was younger, and my Dad would jump at the chance to discuss it with me, and use it as a bonding moment. For now, the rusty mallet would have to do.

Gently, I pushed on the metal door that led to the main, open-air section of the fort. Floodlights made the area too bright, almost like a rugby pitch at night. It hurt to stare for too long, at least until my eyes had adjusted.

From a small crack between the frame and the metal, I counted security (four), people I recognised from our group (three, plus one frothing dead on the floor), and how many vehicles were outside (two).

SMASH.

I leapt through the door and quickly felt a stray bullet brush against my arm. It barely grazed me, but I could feel a dragging heat emanate from scolded red skin. A security guard raised his gun to my head, itching to squeeze the trigger. Before he had a chance to, another stray bullet slapped through the soft spot just near his temple, and painted the wall next to us with bloody brain bits.

With seconds to spare, I collapsed into a heap and crawled to a small, hidden area behind the car we'd crashed earlier. The windows were all but shot out, spiky glass shards digging into my knees as I moved. An industrial whirr hissed from above, introducing the mysterious black vehicle from Dad's notes and Leo's wet dreams. The other times I'd seen it, it was almost supernatural, hovering calmly above us, moving in soft, confident motion. This time, it was struggling to stay in the air, as if desperate to land without any space to do so. A huge section of land to the North started to part, a well-landscaped secret entrance big enough to hold the vehicle.

More people had arrived. I only recognised six or seven of the original group, but now there were easily forty people running around causing mayhem. Plus a dozen more on the floor in different shapes and states, body parts scattered as far as I could see.

"PUT YOUR HANDS ABOVE YOUR HEADS AND GET ON THE GROUND."

A loudspeaker repeated the instruction on a loop, as if saying it twenty times over would change these people's minds. The vehicle above started dipping and rising in a worrying, clunky rhythm, until a small hatch opened on the underside, revealing the fan I'd seen earlier in the day.

SPLAT.

A disgusting vat of mucus-yellow liquid slopped out of the aircraft, splatting down onto the ground below. The putrid smell wafted through the air, but it was only the start of the plan. One by one, the vehicle hovered above the civilians in the fort, paused for a moment, and then sucked up their bodies, ripping flesh from bone and discarding the entrails back onto the ground. This was the technology whistleblower "Fred" had discussed with my Dad. This wasn't aliens or curious people from the future here to take samples of our flesh-coats, it was our own government, destroying and discarding us for their own gain.

They caused this. All of this. Death and disease and cover-ups.

I'd had enough.

I wrestled the automatic rifle from the dead, spindly fingers of the guard who almost shot me. I checked for the safety, flicked it off, and prayed that some of the conversations with my Dad would put me in good stead for this.

There was a guard in front of me shooting everyone and everything he could see. I brought him into my crosshairs. With a steady intake of breath, I squeezed the trigger, rattling off a heavy spray of bullets in his general direction. A few of them made contact with his face. He was on the floor moments later screaming that he couldn't see any more. I closed the distance between us and popped one more in his skull to solve his problem.

My shoulder screamed in pain, unprepared for the heavy recoil of the weapon. In the distance, I could hear a haunting cacophony of police sirens. The guards looked panicked, and I noticed a stream of men and women in lab coats sprint out of one of the tunnel entrances on the other side of the fort.

Two large trucks emblazoned with 'Lifelong Corp' logos pulled up from a hidden car park. Two drivers jumped out and opened up the back container, allowing the workers to fill it with documents and computers and all manner of shady devices. I turned my rifle to the front wheels, and sprayed a stream of bullets into the tyres. The drivers screamed at me, just as I noticed the aircraft crawl across the horizon, right towards someone waving their hands at it.

I looked closer…

Leo.

"TAKE ME UP! TAKE ME UP NOW!"

No.

The guards had all retreated, running inside the buildings and grabbing what they could to load into the vans. Not that the first one was going anywhere in a hurry. Sirens warbled through the atmosphere, the police gaining on the fort, ready to shut this all down with any stroke of luck. The area outside of the over-illuminated fort pulsated from nighttime abyss to red-blue as the emergency services gained on us.

I heard the chattering of an engine, then a beam of energy shoot from the aircraft. Before I could even think, my weapon was raised, trigger squeezed, pelting the vehicle with the last few rounds of the magazine.

Leo ducked, running for cover.

"IT'S NOT REAL LEO! MOVE THE FUCK AWAY!"

I smelled the smoke before I saw the fire. The buildings choked, heavy plumes escaping from the small grated windows. Desperately, I searched for a way out of this as the vehicle set its sights on me. The floor was littered with dead. Old and young, civilian and security. I couldn't be part of this statistic. And after all I'd been through to help him, I couldn't let Leo be, either.

A small three-door car was parked at a service entrance to my left-hand side. I sprinted towards it, no time to catch my breath or take notice of my burning arm. When I got close enough to touch it, I thanked God and the universe and everyone in between to see the driver dead on the floor, keys entangled in his fingers.

I snapped his finger bones to tease the keys away from his rigor mortis grip, said sorry for being so heavy handed, and heaved his body out of the way. Then I was in the car, keys in the ignition, foot on the accelerator.

"FUCKING TAKE ME NOW!"

Leo was still goading the aircraft. I couldn't fault his commitment to the cause, even if it was complete fiction. The boy had wrapped himself up in complete fallacies, a cult-like obsession with an idea that wasn't even that concrete of an idea in the first place. Blood sacrifices and aliens and spaceships that rip your skin off (although that final one wasn't so far from the truth, I guess).

He was just metres away from the car now, so I pulled over and screamed at him to get in. He looked at me, rolled his eyes, and started to walk away. That really pissed me off.

I got out the car, looked above to see where the vehicle was, and found it had completely fucking disappeared. And then I got really fucking angry again.

"GET IN THE CAR, LEO!"

"FUCK OFF, JOSH!"

He'd dropped his handgun on the floor. I noticed it glimmer whilst we argued back and forth. I swiped it up, and aimed at his head.

"Get in the car."

He laughed maniacally.

"What the fuck are you doing?"

"I'm not losing you," I croaked. "It's all fake. All of it. I can explain, I found my Dad, but—"

Leo turned away, shaking his head. Then span back round just as quickly.

"You still don't believe it? LOOK AROUND YOU, JOSH!"

The sirens grew in pitch. They were so close now.

"There's a way out of this, Leo," I begged. "Come with me now."

He didn't say another word, just shook his head over and over until I felt a red mist appear in front of my eyes.

"Fuck off Josh. You fucking think that you know it all and I want—"

POP.

I fired a round directly into his ankle, which sent him to the floor like a sack of shit. He screamed, swore, and cried, but I didn't have time to comfort him. He tried to kick at me when I went to grab him, but he did so with his wounded ankle and screamed even more. I slapped away his hands and legs as he tried to fight back, then grabbed a handful of his greasy, slicked hair, and made him come with me to the car (or else lose his hair and his life in the same day.)

With a tremendous amount of effort, I managed to stuff him into the backseat and get the car moving before any of the police arrived. I still didn't know how we'd explain this, any of this, but I had Leo back and I was going to save him from himself.

"YOU'RE GOING TO KILL ME! THAT WAS MY ONLY CHANCE! EVERYONE ELSE GOT TAKEN UP, YOU CUNT!"

"FUCKING SHUT UP, LEO! ALL THOSE PEOPLE ARE DEAD. DEAD. NOT UP THERE, NOT IN ANOTHER FUCKING UNIVERSE, THEY'RE DEAD…" I tried to calm myself down. "And *you* got them killed."

I jerked the steering wheel, aligning the front of the car with the gate, which was currently obstructed by several broken bodies. Leo started to punch the seat, grab for my hair, reach to scratch my neck, but I leant forward, avoiding all of his attacks.

"I'M GOING TO KILL YOU, YOU FUCKING CUNT!"

I stepped on the accelerator, speeding dangerously fast towards the entrance. The sirens were so loud now I could practically see the swarm of cars coming our way.

"I'M GOING TO MAKE YOU REGRET THIS, YOU PUTRID SHIT! TAKE ME BACK RIGHT NOW!"

His voice was breaking, throat tight and inflamed and probably red raw on the inside.

I didn't listen to him. Didn't react to his screams or

taunts or jibes, or even the knuckles to the back of my head. I felt the bodies pop under the wheels of the car, and was finally free of that place. I'd let the police find my Dad, then explain everything. Explain-

SMASH.

I felt a heavy thud in the back of my head. In the rearview, I could see Leo had slid down the chair and raised his legs above his waist, and had just kicked me with his good leg. Sirens blared from the left. I saw the police cars in a uniform line, speeding right towards us with full red-blue beams spinning.

It was finally going to be over. Would we finally be safe?

And then—

SMASH.

He kicked me again. An abyss-like darkness fell over my vision, and I passed out on the wheel, still accelerating. The last things I heard were Leo trying the door handle (I'd locked it), the crumpling of broken branches and a serene, peaceful silence, only interrupted by Leo's blood-curdling scream.

I felt the car nosedive from the road off the hill. I felt the crumple of metal as the engine was forced through the passenger side cab, completely obliterating that side of the car. I felt Leo's head collide with mine, a clumsy *smack* that felt wet and deep and probably painful, though pain wasn't something that currently registered.

Then everything stopped. I didn't wake back up for another three weeks.

CHAPTER 31

OFFICIAL STATEMENT: Portsmouth City Council

It has come to our attention that our former subcontractor, *Lifelong Corp LTD*, has knowingly withheld information about secret experiments and other damaging business practices from the council since their initial hiring in 2020. We would like to take responsibility and apologise for the severe hurt and distress the subcontractor caused whilst delivering services for the council, and make it clear that any previous business relationship has been severed with immediate effect.

There is an ongoing enquiry into the extent of damages caused by the subcontractor, and the council is working with all necessary services and co-operating fully with the investigation. The coroner has called for a separate investigation into the deaths of over one hundred and fifty residents, and the council is working with local services to investigate whether there is any pathogenic remnants of the unknown fungal disease in the water supply. We urge all Portsmouth residents to only drink bottled water until further notice. This is available at a discounted rate from all shops in the city.

There will be a number of public information events held across the city in the next couple of weeks for you to put forward your views and concerns with local MPs. Please note that we have no affiliation to the water services nor our former subcontractor Lifelong Corp LTD, so won't be able to answer questions with a direct relation to their practices. However, councillors and MPs will be available to discuss mental health support services, the latest anti-fungal treatments we are trialling for residents infected by the seawater pathogen, and financial assistance for those who lost their jobs at the facilities on Portsdown Hill.

Yours sincerely,
    Ben P. Mourdant
    Council Executive

CHAPTER 32

I faded back to life in the middle of one of the hottest days on record. My clothes were practically skin-tight, the air was heavy, and I could swear I saw the windows sweating. No-one was there to greet me. I doubt anyone had visited.

The nurse was astounded when I woke up, her face beaming as she rushed to get some water and snacks.

"You must be so hungry, there's no good fast food restaurants in dreamland!" She laughed at her own joke.

She came back with a hospital hamburger and chips which looked dry but palatable, and I ate them all in one go.

Between laboured breaths, I listened to a rotating cycle of nurses and doctors talk about how lucky I was to be alive and how, if I hadn't have hit that tree, I would have veered right off the cliff and probably crashed through the roof of someone's house. That reminded me of the scene in *Donnie Darko* with the plane engine, and then I started thinking about parallel timelines and loads of existential shit, so I just asked for more chips to keep my mind off of that.

When all was said and done, and they'd explained everything that needed explaining, I asked the only real question on my mind.

"Did Leo make it?"

— — — —

It was about a month before I got some semblance of normality back. The hospital wanted me in for checkups every few days, to make sure that my brain was still behaving normally after such a heavy accident. They kept reminding me that I was lucky to be alive and shouldn't really be walking and talking now at all. One doctor asked if I believed in God and thanked him for my survival at all. I said no to both parts of the question. If anything, I thanked myself for aiming towards a tree instead of coasting off of a huge hill.

Leo was in bad shape. He was hooked up to a number of things, oxygen and breathing machines and various other devices that beeped and clicked and collected bodily fluid. Trying to cure the infection was the worst thing, I was told (by the same doctor who was big on Jesus). It was unlike anything they'd seen before, and the only real plan they had was to keep trying existing anti-fungal treatments and experimental medicine on him, and hope that it didn't make anything worse. I went in and held Leo's hand a bit, kissed him on the forehead when some of the fungal lesions started to disappear, and read fun stuff from the forums to him in the evenings.

The posts from the last few weeks had been completely wiped. There were no more stories or details about the beach, nor the incidents or the missing people. The government had strong-armed the company into redacting all of the posts, no doubt offering plenty of tax-payer money for the inconvenience. Even my video was taken down, which was mysterious in itself, but I'd had my absolute fill of mysteries. As far as I was concerned, the world could keep its conspiracy theories and secrets and all the shady dealings, and I'd just carry on with my boring little life. I didn't want to be part of anything else.

Six weeks after the accident, Leo was let out of hospital. He still hadn't fully recovered, but they'd found a treatment that was working against the infection. I had a handyman fix up the house with some money my Dad left me in his will, with a hope that maybe it would remind us both of how things were before this all happened. I even got us ramen in mixing bowls and soft blankets to sit on in the living room, but Leo vomited it all up before he was able to finish.

Just like the first night of his infection, I helped him sleep, helped regulate his temperature with damp cloths and hot milk, tucked him in, and reminded him that he was stuck with me whether he liked it or not. He got his sense of humour back towards the start of the seventh week, and had taken to calling me an idiot when I made stupid jokes or suggested that maybe we were actually both in hell right now.

Where the forums had been all but wiped clean in terms of the beach incident, there were several sites on the dark web that were leaking information from various enquiries, doxxing those involved and inviting readers to do their own research and report back with information. I found out a lot from these sites—more information on the shady subcontracting company, the extent of the beach outbreak, some scientific information about the fungus—but there still wasn't any clear explanation of everything we'd seen. With military and government things, it wasn't likely that everything would ever be out in the open, and that made me feel hopeless but also ready to move on.

At around two months after the incident, Leo had a huge relapse. The medicine stopped working, and I had to lock him in his bedroom with food and a bucket to shit in whilst he lost his mind and clawed at the wood, promising that he'd get me and strip off every little inch of my skin before boiling me red raw in the bath. In my mind, I reminded him that the bath had a leak and he'd never get it full enough to cover my entire body. But it wasn't the time for jokes.

A couple of times, I was completely convinced he was lying dead on the floor, but it was a ruse to get me to come in and check on him, before attacking me like a wild animal. I fell for it twice, but both times managed to over-power him and put him back in his place.

The NHS had all but stopped caring about the beach incident, unable to offer any more help until new experimental drugs were ready to go. I asked a receptionist how long that process could take, and she said that it depended on a few factors, but it was usually a few years.

Thankfully, the medicine he had taken before was effective again a few weeks later, and over the next few months, my best friend—the man I was sure I still loved, despite it all—came back in full force. He was funny, witty, smart, cool as a cucumber. One day, he decided he'd had enough of long hair and cut it into a wild, spiky shape, which I thought looked very noughties boy band but was kind of hot too.

We went back to Hayling Island on another camping

trip, and didn't find any dead elderly men or weird people by the sea, but they also stopped doing multipack crisps at the shop, so not everything was better the second time around. Leo and I played drinking games and ate BBQ, almost got frostbite, drank coffee and smoked weed in our tent, and started thinking that maybe we should give the video stuff another go. We could make documentaries about things that interested us, go around the country (and eventually the world) investigating conspiracies, but with enough caution not to get involved in anything first hand. It all seemed like a really fucking perfect plan.

We celebrated New Year and bought loads of equipment from cash saved from odd jobs. We'd identified our first project—mass suicides up in Sheffield with no known cause—and booked hotels and a few people to interview. We fell asleep in each other's arms, and eventually rekindled the spark that had been snuffed out so quickly before.

But then the next day, I woke up to find him missing from the house. Next to a lukewarm cup of coffee, he'd left a note:

I tried so hard to get back to normal, but I need to be there with them. I'm sorry I couldn't be Leo again.

The scribbled note didn't make sense initially: it had been over a year since we'd even spoken about what happened in those few weeks. But the more I thought about it, the more I recalled the lingering stares every time we passed the water, the weird way his eyes would glaze over when something popped up on the news, the way he had to force himself to take the pills as if he thought they were placebos or going to hurt him or something.

I got in my car. The first two places I visited were empty. Not even tourists.

But then I remembered the pier and the arcades and the

first stretch of beach we visited when he came to live with me: the twinkling, nostalgic lights of the arcade, the ice cream stand, the weird little rollercoaster that no-one really rode though it was as much a part of the city as the Spinnaker Tower and drug addiction, so we all just let it be.

When I got out of the car for a third time, I had a feeling I was close. It was a gut feeling, instinct again, promising that I was on the right path and that I needed to hurry up because I didn't like the undertone of that note or the way his mind might have been working at the time. I sprinted over the tarmac until my feet felt pebbles, ushered to the shore by the warm wind. And then I saw him.

He lay on the rocks, contorted and bloody, barely breathing, trousers soaked through with water. There was no-one else around, no-one to help him, no-one to help us. His face was screwed up strangely but not in a violent way; it was kind of peaceful. He looked up and saw me, a smile growing on his face, as if he knew that I would be there despite leaving me the note, like he was happy that I hadn't changed when so many things in the city had. The waves were slowly intruding on the shore, soaking another inch or so of Leo's body each time they returned.

I told him I was going to call an ambulance, but he shook his head and asked if we could kiss. By the time our lips touched, there was no life left in his body, and I noticed the huge gash in his stomach and the knife hanging limply in his right hand. I told him to wake up, because the hotel was booked and I didn't want to let down the interviewees of our new show, and I also didn't want to have to plan yet another funeral. My smart shoes were quite literally worn down from the amount of times I'd had to use them over the previous year.

But when it was obvious that he wasn't go to answer me, I just sat and stared, waiting for someone to pass by and find us. Eventually, I took to screaming, my voice breaking as I begged for help or a miracle or something in between. Nothing came. Nothing ever did.

I gave up any hope of someone coming to see if we were okay, so I called an ambulance and explained what had happened. I told them our exact location and what we were wearing, and that I'd have called earlier but he was definitely dead already. But then the phone signal went funny and I lost them, and it wouldn't dial back.

The air felt cold all of a sudden, the wind completely gone, and when I looked up, I felt a mix of disbelief and relief.

A black vehicle. An aircraft just like the one we'd seen so many times before. I thought it had been explained away, but maybe I didn't know everything and had to be willing to give something else a go.

It coasted above us, taunting, an impossible feat of technology out in the open, ready to take us away. Away from this beach. This city. This relationship. This life. This entire existence.

The last thing I remember is the hatch opening, and an intense buzzing. I squeezed my eyes shut.

THE END

Sign up to Rob's email community for sneak peeks, giveaways, competitions, discounts on merch and the latest in indie horror news.

join.robhorror.com

First Wednesday of every month, no spam, no nonsense. Join now to get a free short story directly to your inbox.

ABOUT THE AUTHOR

Rob Ulitski is a writer based in Portsmouth, UK. Having grown up on a steady appetite of horror films, books and TV shows, he started making films at age thirteen, and working on various film sets in entry-level roles. His writing journey officially started in 2020.

Since graduating from the University for the Creative Arts in Farnham in 2013, he has held a variety of roles, including:
- *Filmmaker*
- *DIY store assistant*
- *Adult (Sex) shop assistant*
- *Writer for a music video blog*
- *Film Festival Organiser*
- *Producer for a Korean TV show startup*
- *Corporate video editor*
- *Photographer*

SOCIALS:
@robulitski

Printed in Great Britain
by Amazon